THE TROUT

PETER CUNNINGHAM

SANDSTONEPRESS
HIGHLAND | SCOTLAND

First published in Great Britain
Sandstone Press Ltd
Dochcarty Road
Dingwall
Ross-shire
IV15 9UG
Scotland.

www.sandstonepress.com

Editor: Moira Forsyth

The publisher acknowledges support from Creative Scotland
towards publication of this volume.

ISBN: 978-1-910985-21-2
ISBNe: 978-1-910985-22-9

Cover design by Mark Swan
Typeset by Iolaire Typesetting, Newtonmore.
Printed and bound by CPI Group (UK) Ltd, Croydon, CR0 4YY

Peter Cunningham is from Waterford, Ireland's oldest city. He is the author of the Monument series, widely acclaimed novels set in a fictional version of his home town. His novel, *The Taoiseach* was a controversial best seller; *The Sea and the Silence* won the prestigious Prix de l'Europe. He is a member of Aosdána, the Irish academy of arts and letters, and lives with his wife, not far from Dublin.

For Carol

We think that we can reach one another but, in reality, all that we can do is to approach and pass each other by.

Franz Schubert (1797-1828)

Part One

Bayport, Lake Muskoka
Ontario, Canada

Two Years Ago

1

Winter, when it leaves Muskoka, often does so over the course of a single night. One evening, darkness falls over a steel grey, ice-bound landscape; next morning, red squirrels, beavers and racoons reappear on the islands and ice quickly becomes a memory. Within forty-eight hours, white-tailed deer can be seen along the shore-line, grazing the groves of maple and hemlock. The lake cottages, shuttered since Thanksgiving, reopen as if a single lock has turned and the accents of Toronto and Detroit can once again be heard in Bayport.

A blue jay, squatting in the lower branches of the oak that stands on the boundary between our garden and the road, is calling to an unseen mate. Soon my room will lose its comforting redolence of books and paper to the fragrance of cut grass and pine. I know I like to deplore the short, cold days of winter, but the truth is that in winter I work best. During four such entombed seasons the story crept from me, word by word, until eventually it lay there in a stack of pages that went on to become a book.

Our house, its foundations blasted into the sheet rock of the Canadian Shield, is built on rising ground half a mile outside the lakeside town of Bayport. Fifteen miles farther west by road, or ten miles by boat, lies Charlton, the district's administrative centre. From our front porch, looking north through stands of white and red pine, birch and oak, Lake Muskoka can be seen: in winter white as bone, in spring—as now—joyfully blue.

Kay walks down the path that runs diagonally to the gate. Tall, with iron-grey hair and strong features, she still moves like a cat. As the blue jay takes off, screeching, she waves a greeting to it, an age-old Irish superstition to deal with the magpie, cousin to the jay.

A small boy with a large, purple rucksack on his back comes up the road, the sun's rays dancing in his black curls. He runs the last few yards to his grandmother, who hugs him, then turns to where she knows I am, as if to say, *Look who's home!*

Up the path they come and the child runs ahead, leaving his grandmother to bring the rucksack.

'Granddad, guess what?'

I show him my puzzled face. 'Tim?'

He takes a flying leap into my arms, grabs my beard with his small fists and buries his head there.

'We won! Our team won!'

4

2

The population of Bayport is 889. Although the town depends on the lakes for its living, in the off-season we still manage to tick over. Bridge clubs and book clubs flourish. Mr Amos, the local grocer, who ties flies for sale in the spring and summer, builds up his stock. The annual production of the town's light opera society is traditionally unveiled at Christmas. Cross-country skiing expeditions thrive. Two churches serve the mainly Episcopalian and smaller Catholic congregations; there is one bar, the Muskoka Inn, and one restaurant, Francini's. The mail for Bayport comes from Charlton, where you go to do banking business, to buy a new shirt or the latest book, or to catch the bus out of Muskoka.

I worked for over thirty years as a teacher of English in Saint Celestine's, Toronto. A lot of teaching. They say it burns you out in the end, or at least, that's the explanation I settled for. When the school appointed a new, young headmaster with fresh ideas, bringing in a new regime, I quit. We sold our house in Milton and moved up here, so I could write full-time. That was all fine until the economic crash came along and took most of our investments with it. Not that we're complaining—we've enough to get by on—but we've had to put travel plans on hold.

Our son, Gavin, Tim's dad, is the palaeontologist with a Canadian archaeological team that's in China for six weeks to do whatever it is they do with the remains of a 200,000-year-old human. Tim's mother died in a pile-up in Toronto when he was three. If there's a school camp going when Tim comes to stay in Muskoka, we enrol him so he can be with kids of his age.

As we sit on the porch with iced teas, the mail van arrives. In some quarters, the late arrival of the mail each day is a major issue: Mr Amos is chairman of a committee whose sole purpose is to have the delivery to Bayport made before noon.

Kay is reading Tim's school camp report, which she found in his rucksack. Birdsong is building along the canopy by the lakeshore. In just two days, the light has soared.

'How's he doing?'

'He's doing fine.' She hands across the single page. 'They say he's got an eidetic memory.'

At a desk just inside the window the child peers at the computer. Tim is dyslexic, of mid-range severity, according to the specialist in Toronto. He also exhibits behavioural idiosyncrasies, with which his father and we have become very familiar.

'I hope enough is being done,' I say.

Kay smiles patiently, as if I'm deliberately missing the point.

'Alex, the man he's seeing is in the top three in North America.'

I know what I want to say. I know whose medical opinion I'd really like to hear on my grandson's condition.

Kay gets up. 'I've got work to do,' she says.

3

The seats of the black Humber Hawk were of stitched red leather, including the rear bench-seat on which I knelt, bare-kneed, inhaling the leather fragrance, surveying the receding world. It was my world, different to what the doctor saw out of the front window: my world at seven years of age, seen through a much smaller frame and going in the opposite direction.

As he drove, the doctor spoke of the power of learning, of the wisdom to be found in books, and of how literature is second in grace only to religion. He spoke in the deep, rich rhythms of Ireland's south-east, his accent one of soft, uvular articulations. The doctor's words, when his humour was good, swirled lovingly around me, but when his humour changed, it changed everything.

The mailbox flap slaps down and the van speeds away. For years, a woman with a pleasant face has done the mail run; she has been replaced and now it seems like a new person every other week. Tiny shoots of growth are bustling either side of the path, luminously green pinheads. For Christmas, Kay gives me a subscription to *The New Yorker*. Once a week, as now, I savour the first glimpse of the magazine's cosmopolitan provenance through its cellophane wrapping.

Jerry Fisher, my literary agent, who initially placed my book with a publisher in Toronto, has promised early news on a sale in New York. No letter has come from Jerry, but there are several for Kay, who works as a psychotherapist in the hospital in Charlton. For our first year up here Kay relished the break from the job that had kept her so busy in Toronto and she threw herself into painting, at which she excels. Her work has been shown in a small gallery in Toronto, where every canvas sold. And yet, because of our circumstances, she feels she cannot rely completely on her painting, which is why she now works part-time in Charlton.

I see a card from Larry White, who has come to live down by the lake in Bayport and is already trying to stimulate interest in next winter's theatrical production. Larry, a former Mountie, arrived here late last year but already sees himself as Bayport's leading man.

Kay is looking out from the porch. Sometimes her glance, as now, contains sadness, as if she is harbouring personal regrets, or fears that our happiness is never more than provisional.

The letter at the bottom of the pile is addressed in type on a brown envelope. A Toronto postmark.

Alex Smyth
Author
Bayport
Lake Muskoka
Ontario

Our postcode. Since the publication of my novel *Sulphur*, I have received three letters, written to me care of my publishers. Two readers called me a hero; the third, a woman in Vancouver, said my book made her physically ill.

In the kitchen, I take the paperknife.

4

According to most dictionaries, the word trout is used to describe a number of species of freshwater and saltwater fish belonging to a subset of the salmon family. The colour of trout reflects the environment they inhabit: in the sea, these fish look silvery, whereas in rivers their appearance is much darker.

By some estimates, fifty-two different trout varieties have been recorded. The brown trout is the only trout native to Ireland. He is among the most aggressive of the species and, as spawning time approaches, he will defend his territory with fury.

'They're *very* excited; they really want to get behind you.'

Two days have gone by and Jerry Fisher has driven from Toronto. His expression is one of keen anticipation as Kay fills his glass from a pitcher of her home-made lemonade. Kay likes Jerry, she told me after she had first met him. Now he gives her a big smile, sips the drink and smacks his lips.

'Thank you, ma'am!'

Jerry is small and round, with a scrunched-up, weather-beaten face from four decades of sailing on

11

Lake Ontario. Whenever he phones me, he uses his tone to convey the reality of my literary prospects. A downbeat opening, *Oh, hello, Alex,* so that at first I wondered if he had suffered a personal misfortune, paves the way for news of rejections; whereas, *Alex!,* a cry of joy, can only mean that the omens are promising.

'Yes, this is a fantastic opportunity,' Jerry says and puts down his glass.

He's been stoking the interest of an editor in a mid-size New York publishing house and now has a contract in his sights. A few days ago I would have relished this news.

'Apart from the money, what will be involved?'

Light bends through the birch trees in a golden arc. Jerry leans forward.

'I guess nobody's going to pay ten grand without a whole host of people in-house committing themselves to promoting you in a major major way. It's what every author at your stage dreams of.'

'What sort of promotion?'

Jerry chuckles.

'They're not going to hand over the money and let you go fishing.'

Fear surges from deep within me.

'Let me think about it.'

Jerry can't hide his surprise. '*Think* about it?'

'I'm quite a private person.'

'I'm sure Alex just wants an idea of what he might be getting into,' Kay says and her green eyes flash as she shoots me a look.

All at once Jerry is uncertain of what's happening.

'It's like what he's done already, only more,' he says to her in a wheedling tone.

What I've done already involved an article in the *Charlton Gazette*, an interview with a Vancouver-based literary magazine and a tiny get-together—launch would be ridiculous—in a bookshop in Toronto, where twenty people drank budget wine and I signed some books. Jerry begins to describe what a low-to-mid-level publicity campaign in New York might require.

'You grew up in Ireland, right? I mean, how else could someone write a great book like this? That whole business about the boy out fishing with his father—unforgettable. *That's* what they want to hear!'

5

The shrimp is a shy and furtive creature that lives on the riverbed. Greenish in colour, it clings to stones with its tiny legs, back hunched, its head down. When the trout wants a shrimp that is crawling along the bottom of the river, he must shovel it off with the flat side of his mouth.

The lake is still bright at Roger's Quay, where for years I have rented a covered berth—a space in a long shed on a jetty with an electric hoist to lift my boat clear in winter.

Jerry had left earlier. Although we'd agreed to meet soon in Toronto, it was obvious he was unhappy. I helped Kay tidy away the glasses.

'I'm going to check the boat,' I said, but she turned away. 'What's wrong?'

'What's *wrong*? What's wrong is that we sold up in Toronto and came here so that you could write. Now most of our savings are gone, but when you get the kind of break we were praying for and your agent comes to talk about how to promote you, you act like you're autistic.'

Beneath the spaced wooden jetty boards, the water twinkles. Boats are still coming in from the islands.

This place is cold and dead in winter, but from now on it will sing with activity.

A man emerges from a berth. He is broad-shouldered, dressed in blue overalls, and his ink-black hair is tied in a ponytail, the way a lot of the Ojibweys wear it. I've never been able to gauge Keith's age from his deeply creased brown face, but he has to be at least fifty.

'Mr Smyth.'

'Keith, how are things?'

'Good.' Keith is a man of few words. 'Boat's all set.'

He can turn his hand to anything, the opposite of me. On his time off, for a few bucks he'll come over and do odd jobs around the house.

'I might take her out later,' I say.

'Keel's good as new.'

Maid of Kerry, my white-hulled, twenty-foot launch, has high bows, a spray-hood and a windscreen. Forward of the cockpit is a semicircular bench done in imitation white leather. The head of a ninety-horsepower Evinrude shines above the stern.

'Looks great.'

'Thanks,' Keith says.

There's a story from way back about how Keith once did time in a juvenile prison, south of Chatham on Lake Erie, for trafficking in contraband cigarettes. Seems he worked there on a boat for old Danny Forman, whose son now owns the business here in Roger's. When Keith got out of prison, Danny gave him a job.

'Seen any strangers?' I ask casually.

Keith's dark eyes fasten. 'A few cottage people back.'

'But no one hanging around.'

'You expectin' someone?'

15

There's another dimension to Keith, a different person who occasionally steps into view.

'You know that book I gave you?'

'Sure.' Keith scratches his head. 'Kinda started it, but . . .'

'Sometimes you get reporters. Trying to find out about writers, looking for a story.'

'You goin' to be famous, Mr Smyth?'

Something mocks in Keith's slow smile.

'Hope not. But you never know—you could get someone poking around.'

'Want me to keep a lookout?'

'Just in case.' I make myself smile. 'Best be ready.'

'Like they say,' Keith says, 'no smoke without a fire.'

6

Put yourself into the mind of a trout, braced against the current of the river, two fathoms down. Suddenly, up in the bright air dome something changes: a shadow splits the light above your head. What do you do? Memory deep as oceans clutches at you. All you can think of is survival. What do you do? You do nothing. In the cool recess of the bank you wait. You sit it out. If you stay down here the danger will disappear. You do nothing.

Kay lifts her easel from the box room where it has spent the winter, and her palette, and brings them out to the porch with a canvas, a box of paint tubes, brushes and white spirit. Tim is with the Echenozs, our neighbours, whose son, Pierre, is eight years old. The wind has gone south. Across the fence Dimitri Echenoz is barbecuing.

Over the years Kay has tried to paint indoors, but has never liked it. And whereas she seldom paints what she sees, her thickly layered and richly coloured oils hailing from deep in her psyche, it is only out of doors that she can find her stimulation. She spins the wing-screws that adjust the easel's legs, secures the canvas, assembles the brushes and jars on a low table and begins.

As she paints, she tries to relax. She has been worried about our marriage for some time. Over the years, when I have become depressed, when an inner turmoil has overcome me, when I have been prey to nightly panic attacks and feel I am being suffocated, she has urged me to go into analysis, but I have always resisted. When Gavin, our son, grew up and we moved to Milton, we both had careers that ate up our days and often our weekends, but we valued our time together. We were financially secure. That was before I took early retirement. Now, in Muskoka, we spend most of our days under each other's feet and have to watch every dollar. We seldom have sex more than once a month.

She thought that writing the novel would be a catharsis for me, that it would amount to a form of self-analysis that might help me come to terms with my problems. It seems the opposite has happened; I have become even more eccentric. Today with Jerry Fisher was a new low, as if I had deliberately placed at risk everything I have worked towards. Kay grits her teeth. She doesn't know how much longer she can take it.

Since we moved to Muskoka, our lives have become more isolated. At least in Toronto we had professional friends and colleagues, but here, in this lake wilderness, she realizes, there is no one to turn to.

When she begins to paint, Kay seldom does so with any fixed idea. Even at the moment when the loaded brush meets the canvas, her mind is divided: one part guides her hand, the other sorts, analyses and files away matters that until now were circling in the air.

She extends the line downwards in a graceful curve.

We got married when we were nineteen years old, children, something she often thinks about now and wonders once more if our decision was a mistake. Neither of us knew anything about life, or what we did know amounted to so little. She wonders about the huge gamble we took and, in the process, the great potential she may have left behind.

Her father died when she was a child. A big strapping man, rowing on the river had been his sport. She keeps a photograph of this young man of splendid physique, in a singlet and shorts, one of a crew of eight, standing on the Ferrybank side, the Suir their backdrop. One morning he stood up before a class of twelve-year-old boys and, as he began to chalk a mathematical equation on the blackboard, fell down dead. He was thirty-nine years old and a brain aneurism was discovered in the post-mortem.

The priest told her that God had wanted her father for special business in heaven. When God calls someone, that is the greatest honour that anyone can ever receive, the priest said. Kay knew that there had been a mistake, that God would never take her dad when he was also needed so badly at home.

At times of difficulty, like these, she sometimes tries to imagine her life without me. What would it be like? She would have buried her mother and watched her younger sister die of cervical cancer at the age of forty. Lived in the house in Waterford that her father had bought when she was born. Never become an outsider, which was how she felt at her sister's funeral, like she often feels in Canada.

Freedom and a sense of puzzled excitement seize her with these old thoughts. She wishes she could see clearly into my soul, for even though she once trusted me, now she is not so sure. Everyone has secrets, she reflects, as under her hand a human form takes shape; this emerging image has its secrets, which it will share with me alone. Her brush has been moving continuously and now she pauses, sits back and the air is sucked from her. The moulded back of a power-fully built man springs from the canvas, the long twin muscles diving down into the mystery of his waist. He is beautiful. Kay bites her lip. She savours him achingly until she can no longer bear it, then she takes a palette knife and scrapes the whole thing away.

7

The doctor's residence on the outskirts of Carrick-on-Suir was entirely consistent with professional integrity and social standing. A cow and her calf grazed beneath two-hundred-year-old beech trees on the property's five acres; the River Suir ran along the bottom of the land. The doctor's patients were seen in the front room where, for a few short years, my mother had entertained.

Every morning, at seven o'clock, his day began at the local church with Mass and Holy Communion. Days ended in his study, where, having written up his journal, he poured himself a whiskey. For hours we spoke of fly fishing. How to cast, and where; the best rods to buy; the wiles of those trout he'd almost caught; how to judge water; how to make a variety of dry flies. Christ was a fisherman too, you know, he'd sometimes tell me, with a smile.

Over the years, I've been medicating for high blood pressure. It comes and goes, like a current in my mind, rising and falling. Alone, I listen to the wind in the roof, gnawing at the shingles like a dog at a door. The whiskey hits the back of my tongue.

Maybe I'm being paranoid. Maybe it's the kind of man I have become.

'We need to talk,' Kay says and turns off the television.
  'Fine.'
She removes her spectacles and places them on the table beside her. The grey is spun through her hair like chalk seams through slate.
  'What is it?' she asks.
My instinct is to brush her off. 'What do you mean?'
  'I mean, what's happening? First of all, you send Jerry away wondering if he's wasting his time with you. Ever since, you've been going around like a zombie. You're drinking too much and swallowing blood pressure pills like M&Ms. What's going on? If I didn't know you better, I'd say you were having an affair. Maybe you are—are you?'
I shake my head and pretend to laugh.
  'It's not funny! You have this look on your face all the time. What *is* it?'
A large tabby cat that belongs to the Echenoz family has come to sit on our windowsill.
  'Nothing... nothing at all.'
  'Come on, Alex! We need to work this out, whatever it is.'
I take a big breath. 'Look, I'm trying to come to terms with something, okay?'
  'With what?'
  'It's very far back and deep down...'
We sit in throbbing silence.
  '... one moment it's there, the next it's out of reach. Gone. I think I'm afraid.'

'Why?'

'I don't know. Once, years ago, I tried to tell someone, but they wouldn't listen. Maybe I'm just a coward, afraid to try again.'

Kay takes a deep, impatient breath. 'You're not a coward. But let's stay with that. What did you try to tell someone years ago?'

'I'm not sure. I have to try and get my head around it.'

She does this for a living, listens to people like me who are trying to get their heads around their lives.

'I wrote a book.'

'I know.'

'But it wasn't true.'

'It was fiction, Alex.'

'It was a eulogy to my father.'

'Okay.'

'There's stuff… I was a child.'

'When we are young we often have encounters that leave us deeply marked,' she says after some moments. 'There's nothing to be ashamed of. A child is innocent.'

'This was different.'

'We all think we're different.'

'No, this was *different*.'

Another pause as she shows me her patient, professional side.

'Tell me why it was different.'

I get up and stretch; my back has begun to hurt. 'The truth is that my father didn't deserve a eulogy.'

'You can't spend your life blaming your father for everything.'

'I sometimes have bad dreams that I can't remember,

and yet I remember the feeling of the dream, tiny snippets, like a smell, or a flavour that reminds me of something from long ago. It's as if my memory has big holes in it.'

'What's brought this on now? Is it Jerry?'

'No, of course not.'

'What, then? Some event? Something you read?'

'No.'

This is my first outright lie.

'What then?'

'I need time.'

'I can help you. Tell me.'

'I'd like to, but... but that's it for now.'

'It's not very much.'

'I'm just not ready yet. I'm sorry.'

'So am I,' she says and fixes me with a cool look.

'What do you mean by that?'

'I said at the outset, we need to work this out.'

'So you interrogate me?'

'This is a discussion between a married couple, not an interrogation.'

'It sounds to me like an interrogation and I don't feel like continuing.'

'And I don't feel like living under the same roof as someone who's behaving the way you are,' she says.

Perhaps it's the whiskey, but I say: 'Well then maybe you should find someone else's roof to live under.'

The blood drains from her expression.

'What did you say?'

I'm trembling. 'I can't help being the way I am. If that doesn't suit you, perhaps we should rethink things.'

'Maybe we should!' she cries and springs to her feet. 'Maybe that's exactly what we should do.'

24

8

All trout eat each other, including females, who regularly consume their young. In the case of the alpha male, the choice and preferred size of prey is an adolescent fish, one-third of the predatory trout's body-length.

Tim is already in his wetsuit. The sky over Roger's Quay is clear blue and the young maple trees on the shoreline are holding the sun in their fledgling leaves. Way up in the thermals, a hawk is pinned. We walk out along the warm boards to the covered berth. Keith is working on a boat, out on the water. He waves. Tim waves back. The boat's engine fires and I loosen the painter. Sometimes, in the mirror, particularly when I am tired, or upset, as I am now, I see the doctor. Then I get a fright, and realise I must have been afraid of him. North-east of Roger's Quay there's not much traffic and it's sheltered from southerlies.

'Hermit's Island's up this way,' Tim says.

'How do you know that?'

'I know lots of things.'

'You been there?'

'Maybe.'

'I see. So why's it called Hermit's Island?'

'Keith says an old Indian once lived out there on berries and cigarettes.'

'That's all he lived on? Come on!'

'Okay, I guess he also ate stuff like rabbits, birds' eggs, lake weed, wild potatoes, bark, perch, trout, roots...'

'Okay, okay.'

The child's laughing face is bathed in sunlight. The engine idles as he jumps over the side and fumbles on his skis. I'm so proud of him. I didn't learn to swim until I was thirty.

'Ready, Granddad!'

Forward throttle.

Deep in the river, you flex your body with the stream, waiting for the shadow to disappear. This is your hunting ground, your private realm, the place you live and feed and reproduce in. Every fibre in your body shimmers. The light above your head slowly changes. Sooner or later, you will have to rise.

Tim gets up on the third attempt. On a wide expanse of empty water between islands, I keep the boat on a due-east heading so the sun won't blind him. Either side of us, between the islands' pine trees, figures sometimes move, dark, gliding shapes, people I have never met.

A boat comes up behind, wide out on our port side; the skipper waves. It's Larry White, on his way to fish off one of Muskoka's many islands. Larry's a tall, athletic man, around my age, with penetrating blue eyes and a head of full, dark hair. Last year, shortly after he arrived in Bayport, he and I found ourselves side by side on a ten-mile cross-country ski-hike for a children's charity. For most of that day he said nothing, but then, as we trudged through snow-sagging pines, Larry suddenly told me that in cases of spouse murder, the police always start with the surviving party. The remark surprised me, for it came out of nowhere and made me wonder at Larry's mindset.

I wave back as his boat keeps a north-east bearing and we head for home. Illuminated foam flies over the bows as we gently thud-thud across the wake we made in the turn. Tim is a study in concentration.

9

The moon has begun to wane. Kay looks up from her desk and out of the single window of her ground-floor office in Charlton Hospital. It's nine-thirty and her last patient has just left. Across the gardens, in the wire-fenced hospital parking lot, the yellow lights have come on. She lays her hands out flat before her. It happens the whole time, she thinks: people walk away when they have nothing left to say, even after forty-plus years.

She lays her head down on her arms and begs the night to claim her. She can remember exactly the first time she saw me: where she was, who she was with, the lovely waft of ozone on the air, laughter coming from the sea. She was on her half-day, with two other girls who were also trainee nurses, and they had taken the bus out to Tramore. Anything than spend another afternoon with her mother in a house of interminable sadness. When they got off the bus and walked towards the sea, a group of youths outside the slot machines had whistled, and the girls had laughed as they pretended not to hear.

The sea breeze blew their skirts tight to their legs as they walked the length of the strand, well over a mile from the town. She felt young and suddenly liberated. She belonged with the lazy gulls floating high over the waves, in an element she could feel but not yet imagine. She could look down and see this tall, slender girl, so full of beauty, her whole life before her, a speck on the long strand. Her arm was caught; her two companions had stopped and were looking into the sea where a large group of boys were thrashing.

'Look! Some of them can't swim!' her friend giggled and the three of them had doubled up.

Kay gets up and walks to the water cooler by the window of her office. With a plastic cup she stands, watching the night as it slowly inks out the shrubs and flowerbeds and leaves the wire fence of the parking lot like an illuminated prop on an empty stage.

She can tell that Larry White, the former Mountie, is attracted to her. At first, she thought nothing of it, since, like any good-looking woman, she has long known how to deal with such advances. Yet, when she met him a week ago in the aisle of the supermarket in Charlton, and Larry made her laugh about something—now she can't even remember what it was—she came home that night and lay in bed with a tingling want in the base of her stomach.

She refills the cup and presses her forehead to the cool window. Larry, who is without a wife, looks younger than his years. His body is lean, his hands strong, and when he sees her he seems to recognise something that I have forgotten, she will later say. Of course, nobody knows where he comes from, or what he did in the Mounties, or why he now lives in Bayport. Larry is a man with no past and, for reasons she cannot understand, Kay finds that attractive too. She makes herself breathe deeply, closes her eyes, opens them again and looks into a man's face at the other side of the window glass.

She leaps back and gasps. She screams. A man seems to be stuck there. His gaze follows her. Kay reels, turns, grabs the telephone receiver and punches out a number.

'Security.'

'This is Kay Smyth.' She makes herself turn again to the window. 'There is . . . .'

'What is it, Mrs Smyth?'

The window is empty. Kay is shaking violently.

'A man . . . a man has just been outside my window.'

'In, uh, in A3?'

'Yes, but he's gone now.'

'Stay in your office, ma'am. Lock the door. I'll be right there.'

She cannot bring herself to go over and lower the blinds. She stumbles out to the corridor, its walls white, the sterility of the hollow space suddenly chilling. Silence hums. She shrinks into the doorway of the washroom, unwilling to enter and lock herself in a cubicle, unable to bring herself to leave the building. The door is open to her office and from where she stands she can just about see the window. There is no one there.

His face was distorted, the way he pressed it against the glass, or he might have disguised it, for it seemed unnaturally pale. If he was one of her patients, she would recognise him, although she sees no one from the high-risk end of psychiatric pathology. In all likelihood it was a vagrant, or a drunk, who has wandered into the hospital grounds and been drawn to her illuminated window. The recession has played havoc with people's lives. Kay breathes more evenly. She does not want the security guard to find her cowering in a door-well. She returns to her office.

No more than a few minutes have elapsed. The guard, whose desk phone is probably patched through to a mobile device, could be anywhere in the grounds. He could be outside in the garden. Kay's window is empty; the bare fence of the parking lot stands out starkly, cutting up into the black silky belly of the night.

She forces herself to sit. Part of her wonders if by any chance she has imagined the incident. The fact that she has always been superstitious, even as a child, seems highly relevant: she still watches horror movies through the slits of her fingers.

'Mrs Smyth?'

Kay starts. A youngish man with a round face is standing at the door. He is wearing a dark uniform and cap and holding a night stick.

'You okay, ma'am?'

'I'm fine now, thank you.'

'Want to tell me what happened?'

She relates, calmly, how she was standing by the water cooler and looked up at a man. 'He was pressed right up against my window.'

The security guard is taking notes. Kay is not sure she has seen him before: security is contracted to a firm whose personnel seem to change regularly. She describes the man at the window as best she can, then asks, 'Have you checked the grounds?'

'Going to right now, ma'am. Wanted to make sure you were okay first.'

He looks at his notes.

'You certain there was someone? You know, sometimes our eyes play tricks.'

'I'm very sure, yes.'

'I'll write a report. You can see it when next you come in.'

She watches as he makes his way back down the corridor, checking each door. Her desk locked, she gathers her bag and keys, and then goes over to the water cooler. If she leans towards the window, like so, there is unquestionably a reflection. As she looks left, then right, the reflected image follows her. Kay sighs and wonders. She needs a vacation; it's been three years since the last one. She leans in, pressing her forehead to the cold glass. She starts. This close, the image is pale and blurred. Kay straightens up, critical of herself. Down the hall, the security guard has checked the washrooms and is proceeding to the exit. Could it possibly have been him, Kay wonders, as she switches out her light? He could well have been out patrolling the gardens. Why did it take him so long to get to her? As she steps out of her office and is closing the door, she stares. Outside her window a man is looking in.

'*He's there!*' she screams. '*There!*'

The guard hurries back to her. The window is empty.

'He was just *there!* He's *outside!*'

The guard dashes down the corridor, Kay behind him. Outside, as they round the end of the building, the distinct sound of an engine starting up can be heard.

'Hell!' the guard cries. 'He's taking off!'

He sprints ahead, flat out, to the parking lot, where a white Chevy pick-up is pulling out. The guard runs in front of it, his hands out, and the truck stops.

'Stand back, ma'am!'

Kay is open-mouthed. The man climbing down from the truck is Larry White.

10

Some nights, when the day had not gone well, when a patient who should have lived had died, the doctor drank whiskey thirstily. On such nights he spoke in low, haranguing tones about the scourge of tuberculosis, the medical deficiencies he encountered on a daily basis, and about the widespread injustice of poverty.
I sat, not daring to leave. I was small, thin and inclined to get colds easily. At school, I was often picked on. My inability to thrive, the doctor said, was because I had lacked the breast.

As he spoke, my father's jaw became rigid. More than once, he dashed his tumbler into the red coals of the fire grate. When the glass was full of whiskey, a ball of shimmering fire shot up the chimney.

Larry White is sitting in my chair. He's drinking coffee. It's eleven-thirty at night. Kay sits forward, hands in her lap, avoiding me. Larry is wearing a short-sleeved t-shirt that shows his arms are in good shape and he smells of aftershave. All at once, everything about him is physical.

'Describe him again,' Larry says.

'Tall, pale.' Kay takes a drink from her glass of

hot whiskey. 'Very pale, but that could have been the lights. Intense.'

'How big was he? Big as me?' Larry asks.

'Maybe, although he was wearing a coat, so it's hard to say.'

'A coat?' Larry says, making the garment immediately suspicious.

'Maybe he was trying to hide the clothes he was wearing beneath it,' Kay says.

'Such as?'

'I don't know. A uniform? I don't know.'

The west wind has got up again and is sighing softly in the loose roof shingles. From the lake comes the looping hoot of an owl.

'It's funny the way your mind plays tricks. For a moment, until the second appearance, I thought he might have been the security guard.'

At the dresser I pour myself another whiskey. Larry looks down at the notebook I now see lying in his lap. His presence annoys me, for although he trailed Kay's car all the way home, just to be sure she was safe, as he put it, the fact that he has taken over the questioning here in my house makes me irritated.

'Any idea what's going on?' he asks me quietly.

I look first to Kay. We have barely spoken in several days.

'Me? No, I have no idea.'

'Let's try and have a look at him,' Larry says and lifts the lid from a box.

Larry was in the hospital earlier, visiting a friend, he told me. A spotlight in our rafters shines on his face and I suddenly see how smooth the skin on one side of his jaw is, as if someone has layered it on there. He has taken strips consisting of lips and hairpieces, noses, eyes and eyebrows from his box, and is shuffling them around a stencilled head until a pale, round-chinned man with longish hair begins to appear.

'Older,' Kay says. 'Darker hair.'

'Looks like a Halloween monster.'

We all look up. Tim, in pyjamas, has been sitting at the top of the stairs throughout our discussion.

'Hey, little guy! You doin' okay?' Larry chuckles.

'You should be in bed, Tim,' I say.

'May I please have a juice?'

'No, go to bed.'

'Please, Granddad . . .'

Kay's head snaps upwards. 'Will you for once do as you are told? Go to bed! Now!'

We sit in a pool of raw silence. Kay and I scarcely know each other anymore.

'Let's keep going,' Larry says as Tim disappears. 'I once did this a lot.'

My annoyance at Larry's involvement is replaced all at once by a new fear: what if, staring up from the bits and pieces of human physiognomy, I see myself? This crazy thought has no basis in reason, yet it suddenly seems an appalling possibility. I'm perspiring and realise that Larry will not miss this fact. I want him out of my house.

'I think we should get in touch with the police in Charlton,' Kay says.

'Okay.' Larry nods. 'I can make contact on an informal basis; ask the guys to run this composite through the system.'

I've seen the way he looks at Kay. We've joked

about it: *Hey, you know why these guys are called the Mounties?*

'It sounds to me like it was one of your patients,' I say.

She looks at me coolly. 'I *know* my patients.'

'Someone who stopped seeing you, maybe years ago. He's older, sicker. You wouldn't recognize him, especially at night, through a window.'

'No, I don't think so.'

'Surely it's a possibility.'

'How about you, Alex?' Larry asks.

'What about me?'

'Do you recognize him?'

They're both looking at me.

'I have no idea who this person is,' I say.

11

'You have to get badness out,' the doctor said as he explained why a seemingly healthy young woman had to undergo an operation. 'It may lie under a tooth, or under a toenail, or it may lurk deep down in your gut, but in the end it has to come out.'

'Why, Daddy?'

'Because that's the nature of badness.'

One moment, as he drove, the doctor was telling me of the drugs they have in America that Ireland could not afford. A moment later we have driven onto the grass margin, he's pulled on his waders and we're walking down through a field of Friesian heifers.

'When you come to a stretch of water for the first time, never rush at it. Take your time. Study the plants, the animals and the insects. This is their world and you've just invaded it.'

Upriver from Carrick, I sat on the riverbank, sucking bull's-eyes, and watched him cast into a sluggish flow.

'In rising water the fishes tend towards the middle of the stream, but, if water is falling, they hide under the banks or the bushes.'

The split-cane rod flexed and the doctor chortled. With graceful sideways movements, nearly up to his waist in water, he drew out a two-pounder, scooped the trout into the net, and laid him, flapping, on the grass bank. Dripping, the doctor put down the rod and turned to me with a grin. In his hand was a lead-tipped leather cosh.

'You know what this lad is called, Alex?'

Before my astonished gape, with a single blow he killed the fish.

'This,' the doctor said as he straightened up and shook the cosh, 'is the lad you need when someone is really sick. He's called the priest.'

The first part of the road to Toronto twists around lake inlets and acres of naked black rock. I bought the car, an old Wolseley, just for its real leather seats with their bouquet of memory, and over one winter helped restore her with the owner of an auto repair shop in Charlton.

I was very good at teaching, at conveying the passion I felt for literature into the heads of sixteen- and seventeen-year-olds. Yet, sometimes in front of a class, looking down at the rows of open, trusting faces, I was seized with shame for something I didn't really understand, as if shame swam in my blood without the need to account for itself or explain its origin.

At Gravenhurst, I join the highway. I am relieved at being on my own, at not having to keep up pretences. My cell phone chimes as I near Toronto's outer ring.

'Hi. I'm nearly there.'

She likes me to call when I arrive.

'Pull over, then call me back.'

'Pull over?'

'Just do it.'

She hangs up. My first thought is: Jerry has written to say he's going to withdraw. But would he have done that if he knew I was coming to see him? There's a slip road into a shopping mall. I sit, listening to the traffic on the highway, watching families at picnic tables outside a coffee shop. A man on an island of green throws a ball for his dog as the skyline of the city, somehow alien, looms. My cell phone rings.

'Are you off the road?'

'Yes, I am. I was just going to—'

'Something's going on.'

12

Within the brown envelope addressed to

Alex Smyth
Author
Bayport
Lake Muskoka
Ontario

I'd felt something knobby. I slit the seam, withdrew a sheet of folded tissue paper and opened it. What at first looked like a small, green insect with a black head, pale hackles and pink translucent wings lay there. Then I saw the tiny hook, curved and pointed, like a golden phallus.

The envelope and its contents are now in the bottom drawer of my filing cabinet.

Clouds scud over, the traffic hums. I've sat for over thirty minutes, parked outside the highway coffee shop. The man throws the ball for the dog. Every time the dog jumps, the sun illuminates its fur.

This morning, Tim and Pierre went into Bayport to return a DVD, Kay told me. As they were walking home, uphill from the lake, about a hundred yards from our house a pick-up truck was pulled in. The man behind the wheel turned around when the boys came level, then started up and drove away. Tim says he's the man in Larry's box.

What would it be like if I disappeared? People do so the whole time. *Author Disappears*. Would Jerry be happy or annoyed? When I called him and told him I couldn't make it today, he sounded acutely displeased.

13

For my seventh birthday, the doctor gave me a finely bound copy of *Robinson Crusoe*. Although I tried to read it, the print was small and the gist of the story, which I had previously seen in coloured storybooks, dense and impenetrable. What I much preferred were comics, with cowboys, or coaches that were ambushed by highwaymen. The doctor did not approve of comics and refused to let me buy them, but a boy in my class, Seán Phelan, gave me his when he had finished them and I smuggled them home in my lunch box.

After a few pages, I put down *Robinson Crusoe* and lay back, thinking about places we had visited that day, such as the Clonmel tenements that lay in rows beneath the high wall of the industrial school. The windows in the building above the wall were made fast with iron bars, and the shouts of the boys locked in there drifted up into the hazy day.

As night falls, Kay sits at the kitchen table with a stack of files.

'Would you care for tea?' I ask.

'Tea would be good.'

It pains me to see her put to the trouble of reliving

her past encounters with patients in order to bridge the unbridgeable. And yet, like a gambler down to his final long shot, I can imagine her jumping to her feet, a file in her hands, and crying, *I think this is him!*

Kay called Larry when Tim told her about the man in the pick-up. Larry was nearby, so he came over and spoke to the cops in Charlton. However, as no crime has been committed and since the image from Larry's Identikit has not been cross-referenced to a known criminal, their interest is understandably low-key.

'I want to apologise,' I say. 'I behaved badly the other day. I said things I shouldn't have said and which I didn't mean. I am very sorry.'

Kay nods slowly. 'Thank you.'

'I know you were only trying to help.'

'Yes, I was.' She takes a deep breath. 'I've been thinking.'

'About…'

'The man at my office window,' she says. 'The same man Tim says was sitting outside on the road.'

'Tim is just a kid. He's only seven.'

'He's got a photographic memory, Alex.'

'Okay. Let's say it is the same man.'

Kay bites her lip. 'This is probably silly, but do you think it could be Larry?'

I stare at her. 'Larry?'

'Two incidents, and both times Larry shows up immediately afterwards.'

'You called him—the second time.'

'And he shows up in, like, two minutes?'

'You mean, he could be…'

'Stalking me, yes.'

'Jesus.'

We sit looking at one another, as if we've just opened the door and let something alien into the room.

'I've seen the way he looks at me,' she says.

'Larry... was a cop.'

'He *says* he was. What do we know about him? Nothing. He could be sick, he could be... anyone. Believe me, I know what goes on in some people's heads. It's terrifying.'

I can see Larry's face, under the spotlight: he's had surgery that makes his cheekbone shine.

'He comes across as clean and upright,' Kay says, 'but he's a loner. I'm sure he's hiding something.'

I'm assailed by a sudden series of images, stretching over an arc of years, beginning with a dark, tousled head on an Irish summer's day and ending with Larry White's face.

14

The boiling water hisses. My hand is steady as I pour.

'I don't know who Larry White is,' I say. 'He got here—what? Five months ago? Six?'

'You sure you never met him before? I mean, way back?'

'I'm not sure of anything.'

'So he *could* be someone you once knew. People change. I met a woman at a conference a couple of years ago. Until she told me I was in school with her, I had no idea who she was.'

She likes her tea weak so I pour her cup first.

'Kay, I'm going to try and explain something.'

She's looking at me calmly.

'A long time ago, when I was a child, things happened that I've been burying ever since. It involved another boy... my age.'

'When you say, things happened...'

I must concentrate on each word. 'I think I murdered someone.'

Kay doesn't flinch, doesn't move. We sit without speaking for so long, I wonder if she's still there, even though I can see her.

'I see,' she says eventually. 'Want to tell me about that?'

'I can't tell you because I don't remember. I've tried but I can't. It's like there are big holes in my brain.'

'But you *murdered* someone.'

'It's more a feeling than a real memory. Layers and layers... I know I did it, yet I don't know why I know it.'

Once, on a plane heading west, my first sight of the North American landfall made me weep with gratitude.

'Who did you murder, Alex?'

'I don't know.'

Kay makes a point of drinking her tea.

'You mentioned there was another boy. Did you murder him?'

'No, definitely not.'

'What was his name?'

'Terence.' It's been nearly fifty years since I've said his name. 'Terence.'

'Terence who?'

'I don't know. I never knew his second name.'

'You weren't in school with him?'

'No.'

'What happened to Terence? Afterwards?'

'He... went away, I think.'

Her expression indicates that she's trying to understand. 'So you think he could be the person at my window? The man who was sitting outside our house?'

'It's possible.'

'Why would he do that?'

'I don't know. Maybe he read my book.'

'And...'

47

'He saw that he was wronged in the book. Ignored. He came looking for me.'

'Yet it was *my* window he came to.'

'I know.'

Kay looks at me narrowly. 'Do you recognise Terence from Larry's composite?'

'No.'

'Is Terence Larry?' Kay asks.

This new possibility is making my head spin. 'My memory of Terence is very faint—I think I met him only once or twice.'

'Larry arrived here last fall.'

'Yes, and my book came out a few months before that.'

'You and he are around the same age,' she says.

'But Larry's from Vancouver.'

'He told you that?'

'Actually, he told Keith.'

'And as far as anyone around here knows, you're a retired teacher of English who's lived his whole life in Toronto.'

Once, at five in the morning, there was a beaver, right out there next to our gate: you see things for the first time and you wonder where they've been hiding all along.

'Is there anything else you want to tell me?' she asks.

'No.'

'We've never discussed any of this before,' Kay says.

'I know.'

'Alex, it's most unlikely that you murdered someone. Aside from the fact that children don't usually commit murder, if you had done so you would almost certainly

48

have been caught. How old were you? Nine? Ten?'

'Seven.'

'Seven! Come on, Alex! A seven-year-old murderer?'

Her words should comfort me. 'You're right. And yet, whatever it is governs me—the guilt never leaves me. I'm—I don't know what's happening.'

She is beside me. Her strong arms. Blood yaws in my ears.

'Okay,' she says. 'We've got to find out what's going on.'

'I know.'

'Starting with Larry. Is Larry this boy from your childhood?'

'I don't think so.'

I should tell her now about the letter with the fly hook, but the mere thought of it terrifies me.

Kay says: 'We came to Canada, so there's no reason why Terence couldn't have too. Joined the police. So if Larry is in fact Terence, that would explain why he appears to be obsessed with me, but in reality, he's obsessed with you.'

'He's had plastic surgery.'

'I haven't missed that. But there is such a thing as coincidence. It's very simple. We find out who Larry is. This is Canada—there are records, people are entitled to discover information.'

The unfolding inevitability rolls over me. 'Assuming he really was a Mountie, we'll find nothing.'

Kay sighs. 'We could ask him. But if he's taken so much trouble to cover his tracks, he could be dangerous.'

'Shit.'

'We need to be careful.'

A late ferry lets out a warning blast and the lake carries the sound into Bayport.

'There *is* someone who knows what happened,' I say after some moments go by. 'Who knows what became of Terence.'

'Who?'

I look at her steadily.

'Alex...?'

'*He* knows. Or at least he can give me names.'

Kay shakes her head. 'He won't tell you.'

'I have to try.'

She is tight with concern. 'After so much time.'

'I should have done this years ago.'

'It was you he hurt most.'

It's almost too much to contemplate. 'He won't speak to me on the phone...'

Her kindness defines her, as it always has. 'Alex...'

'Tim will be here with you,' I say.

'I'll be fine — it's you I'm worried about.'

'I'll only be gone a few days.'

PART TWO

Ireland

Two Years Ago

1

The connecting plane from London cuts down through two thousand feet of cloud and emerges startlingly close to flooded farmland. A shuttle bus runs to the car rental depot. Ireland's dampness penetrates far more than the sub-zero temperatures of Muskoka where the cold is so intense it makes me cough. Here, five minutes off the plane and I'm shivering.

Heavy rain drenches the south-east motorway. So many years. Cars drive with sidelights on as tide-like water slicks over a highway I never knew existed. On either side, in pastures on which lakes have formed, cattle huddle. Occasionally, the cloud ceiling lifts and a shaft of sunlight picks out a stream, or a hill of gorse in bloom, the bright reflections instantly forgiving their crepuscular surroundings.

A glare on the river is bad, since fish tend to hide under the banks. A murky day is better, but by far the best time to fish for trout is at nightfall.

At two in the afternoon, my heart is clutched by the first sight of Waterford's long quay with its important buildings. The same feeling grasped me, as a child, when we drove in from the country to do our Christmas shopping. If chance had not intervened, I might still be living here, within sight of the water.

The day before, I called the nursing home from Canada and told them to inform the doctor that I was on the way.

'Doctor Smyth? Oh, you mean Paddy.'

He was never called by his first name; 'Doctor' was the only form of address used in three counties, except by me.

As I drive past the Tower Hotel, I recall a tall man in a tuxedo, with slicked-back raven hair, who says the soup of the day is mushroom; but he must be long dead by now. The road out of the city, uphill past the college, is eerily familiar, yet utterly changed with swathes of new houses and shopping malls. A road roundabout has been laid down so that I have nearly passed the turn for Maypark Lane before I realise it. Ten minutes later, in the country, at a crossroads, crossing a tidy bridge over a tributary river, an entrance marked by laurels and rhododendron appears. The doctor had come here once in the old days, when the house was home to a landed family, and had treated the incumbent for gout, a service for which he was never paid, he once told me.

2

Trout tend to rise according to the stages being followed by hatching flies and aquatic organisms. If fish are bulging and darting in weeds and shallows but not breaking the surface, they are usually snatching at nymphs in mid-water. The next stage is when the fish start taking duns on the surface and the third stage is when they go for the spinners.

The object of the fly fisherman is to use flies that mimic each of these stages.

The waiting room is overheated. Every so often I receive a report from the management company into whose bank account I pay a sum each month. The last report I received spoke of 'reduced mobility'. A large young woman in a white uniform hastens in and introduces herself as Mary.

'Can we get you some tea?'

'I'm just fine, thank you.'

'You must be exhausted.'

'No, I'm fine.'

Nurse Mary has a file out, and now, sitting opposite me, begins to go through it attentively. There is some purpose to her that is external to the file, as if the file is a prop. Is he dead? Imagine if he had died even as I was flying here. The dead take away such secrets with them. The nurse looks up.

'Your father is well. He is fundamentally in excellent health for a man of ninety-one. We'll be all lucky to be as good as Paddy, if we get that far.'

'That's good. He's well.'

'Yes, reads the papers, watches television.'

'His mobility is reduced.'

'No more than you'd expect. He sees the physio twice a week.'

'So he can still walk?'

'Oh, yes, he can still walk—but we walk with him.'

'That's kind.'

'Paddy is a very kind man. He is our most long-standing resident.'

What is this woman trying to tell me? Sadness colours the edges of her attitude, and I suddenly understand. Nurse Mary is sad, not for the doctor, but for me. She sighs.

'Mr Smyth, I'm very sorry, but he doesn't want to see you.'

3

When a fish refuses a fly, it can be either because the fly is the wrong size, or has been poorly presented, or because the fish has noticed something that has alerted him to danger.

On most summer nights the doctor went down along the river with Father McVee, the new curate. The priest was tall and broad, with thick black hair and soaring eyebrows that reminded Mrs Tyrrell, our housekeeper, of Clark Gable, she once whispered to me, when the doctor was not listening.

No other person can land such a blow on me; but, then, it has always been so. Nurse Mary's wincing expression conveys her sympathy.

'I did ring your Canadian number, but you'd left. I didn't want to leave a message.'

'He's a very old man.'

'Yes.'

'Perhaps he's not fit to make such a decision.'

'Who knows what he's thinking? But he has his rights too. We can't force him.'

He has rights but he also has responsibilities.

'I want you to give him something.' From my pocket

I take out my book. 'I wrote this. He would like it, I think.'

'Oh!' The nurse becomes temporarily unbalanced by this unexpected development. 'You're a writer.'

'I've written a book, yes.'

'That's wonderful. *Sulphur* by Alex Smyth. Is it a novel?'

'Yes. It will have special meaning for my father. It's about a father and son in Ireland. Their relationship.'

'Oh, my goodness, I never thought you were a writer.' Her eyes are suddenly a nest of clichés. 'I'm sorry, but are you famous?'

'Not at all, but I'd be most grateful if you could give him the book. I'll stay here.'

As she leaves the room, looking back over her shoulder, I go to the table by the window where she has put down her file.

Dr Patrick Smyth, Saint Anne's.
Next of Kin: Alex Smyth,
Bayport, Lake Muskoka,
Ontario, Canada.

I open it and thumb through daily charts of medical jargon and records of bowel movements. Blood type and medication regime. Diet. Exercise and physiotherapy. My telephone number.

I expected his first refusal, since no other course was likely, given the last time. But throughout my childhood the doctor had prided the written word above all else, and urged me to do the same. Now I have written a book. Outside, a slow soft rain slants over the green garden. White seats stand out forlornly. I am ever sucked back to this climate, to this region and its people.

'Mr Smyth?'

She is shaking her head, because she doesn't want me to be hurt a second time.

'I'm very sorry, but Paddy says No.'

Without warning, my legs give. I'm on one knee.

'Mr Smyth, are you all right?'

'I'll be okay.'

'Just take it easy for a minute.'

I can't see properly. 'I am... his only child.'

'I know.'

'He'll soon be dead.'

'I told him he was being silly,' she says. 'I'm sorry. There is nothing more I can do.'

4

The book is on the floor between my feet. The only review I really crave is the one I'm never going to get. I want him to be as caught up in the reading as I was in the writing; but therein lies the flaw. I wrote the book not to tell the truth but to please him.

'Mr Smyth,' she gently touches my shoulder, 'you mustn't blame yourself.'

On my feet. 'I'd like you to have this.'

'Oh, are you serious?'

'Of course. Would you like me to sign it?'

She becomes happily flustered again, fumbling out a pen and spelling out her surname. Signing the title page, I add the date, hand her the book and leave the room.

'Mr Smyth!'

With the heel of my hand I ram into green double doors to my right.

'Mr Smyth, that's not the way out!'

The air in the corridor is stiff with floor wax. Elderly women in pink dressing gowns gape. At the end of the hallway there is a sign: SAINT ANNE'S.

The doctor was slightly built and spry. He wore collar and tie, tweed waistcoat with jacket and matching plus-fours — trousers gathered below the knee, the lower leg clad in a ribbed green stocking — the feet in stout brown brogues. A small, silky moustache ran across his top lip, like a caterpillar.

Sometimes, when he had to leave the car in order to open the gate to a farm, he would spring from nowhere into my vision, thumbs in his ears, his hands spread out to make horns.

Moooooooaaaaaugh!

I loved these impromptu displays of affection, for they swept away my doubts about the doctor and burnished the love that always lay waiting within me. I had come to accept that closeness was a difficulty for him. Unlike the fathers of other boys, he no longer had a wife, and men without wives were different. Mrs Tyrrell, when the doctor was not looking, liked to catch me and kiss me, but she was not my mother, and I knew, and so did Mrs Tyrrell, that because of this the doctor did not approve of such displays of affection.

5

Behind me, the nurse's voice is calling, then fading. Gaudy yellow and orange panels spring out along the corridor, like the inside of a colour-box. My feet resound on the diamond-patterned linoleum. Each room is called after a saint; Saint Anne's is at the end of the corridor.

He is in an armchair by the window, his back to the door, reading a newspaper. This amazes me: that having just judged the thousands of days in which we loved and respected one another as nothing, the doctor can turn to something as banal as a daily newspaper. Clamped behind each of his large hairy ears, like leeches, are flesh coloured hearing aids. I move forward, into his line of vision.

'There is something I have to ask you.'

He looks up and the paper sinks into his lap. So many years have gone by and now it is as if the man I remember has not so much changed as faded. Dressed in a jacket and trousers that I recognize, he wears a blue shirt, slightly frayed at the collar. No tie though. Without the tie, the open neck of the shirt allows sight of his pale, stringy gullet. Large, horn-rimmed spectacles greatly magnify his pupils. He beholds me coldly and moistens his lips.

'I need some information,' I say. 'It's important.'

He tries to speak, but cannot find the words, for he has not expected this intrusion and could never believe that his instructions would be ignored.

'I bear you nothing but goodwill,' I say. 'I am glad you are so well.'

The doctor straightens himself in his chair.

'Have you come to shame your father? Again?'

Mottled brown spots mark his face and the backs of his hands.

'You have a great-grandson. His name is Tim. He will be eight this year.'

A huge urge seizes me to relate the details of Tim's dyslexia, for at my core I believe that of all the doctors in the world, only this old man can fully understand my grandson's condition.

'I think he looks like my mother,' I say instead.

The doctor stares with such astonishment, as if the dead have suddenly appeared, that I want to wrap him in my arms. But he cries out, 'I want him to leave! Nurse! Nurse!'

He attempts to resume his reading, I see with bewildered resentment, although a shake is evident in the spotted hands.

'A name, Dad. From the nineteen fifties. It was a farmyard in the South Riding, all grass—even the way in was a field. Religious iconography everywhere. A husband and wife—the wife was your patient. They had a nephew, about my age. His name was Terence. Something happened. Something bad. Where did Terence go? What was their name?'

The doctor appears not to hear, then his shoulders

rise in the merest shrug of unknowing, or indifference, and he peers at his newspaper as if suddenly absorbed by its contents. My hand sweeps the paper away.

'Fuck you! I'll never see you again, but tell me what I want to know or I'll pray you'll have a hard death.'

Cherries of colour light up his cheeks.

'How dare you come back here! After the shame you brought on me?'

'You hate me because I succeeded where you failed. I wanted your love, but you are only capable of loving yourself.'

The old man's lips curl into a sneer. 'And is that what you put in your... book?'

Trembling, I turn away. 'You will never know.'

At the door to the room, I look back for one last sight of the head I once accepted as being at the centre of my universe.

The doctor says, *'Flannery.'*

6

Mrs Tyrrell cooked, cleaned, set the fires and for six days a week acted as conductor of the doctor's semaphore. Doctor Smyth's practice stretched north to Clonmel, south and west into County Waterford, east into County Kilkenny. He had once worked out that all these little lanes, side roads and boreens that straddled three county boundaries, when added up amounted to an area of two thousand square miles.

A system had begun in my mother's time whereby, if a patient needed attention in Grangemockler but the doctor was on his way from Clonmel to Carrick, a telephone call to the drapery on the corner in Kilsheelin would result in a white flag being placed in the window. The doctor would halt for the flag, telephone home and be diverted to Grangemockler. Since my mother's death, the scheme had evolved into an arrangement involving houses in the three counties. The doctor had even put a map up on the wall so that Mrs Tyrrell, using small coloured pins, could track his daily movements, but she said she knew where he was in her head.

Although it is warm in the hotel bedroom, I shiver. I close the curtains, undress, take my blood pressure

65

tablets, and then stand under the hot shower for five minutes before I call Kay.

'Well?' she asks.

'I just got a name from him, that's all. Otherwise, nothing has changed.'

'I'm so sorry.'

'How are you? That's the main thing.'

'I'm fine—we're fine. Keith is here.'

'I asked him to look at those loose shingles.'

'I'm really fine, Alex. I don't need Keith here to look after me.'

After the call, because I have forgotten to pack my cell charger, I turn off the phone before I get into bed. As I lie, listening to the sounds of traffic on the quay, I realize that even now I'm waiting for a message from the nursing home. *He has changed his mind. He is sorry and wants to see you.* And I would charge out on the road again, full of childish hope, full of love.

The traffic gradually becomes part of the room. *Flannery.* Heavy iron farm gates, high grass, a gigantic alabaster group of statues that includes Jesus dying in his mother's arms. Gnarled thorn trees, like human limbs, stand in proximity to the thatched house, their branches wrapped around with rosary beads, scapulars and the tiny plastic-framed visages of saints.

We are sitting in our new car, a red Humber, and my nostrils are filled with the smell of leather. I look across to my father. He is dressed entirely in black and is wearing on his head a three-peaked biretta surmounted with a woolly tuft.

'You must finish the book,' he is saying to me. 'Then you can come fishing.'

'It's very long, Daddy.'

'Books is all that stands between us and poverty,' he says with the sudden passion I fear most. 'Read it!'

I stare down. The print is small and the lines close together.

AlexSmythAuthorBayportLakeMuskokaOntario

7

Father McVee was a hit with the local country folk who had grown weary of their elderly curate. Now they had a younger man who spoke with passion of God's love, the beauty of the Virgin Mary and the power of the Holy Spirit. Sometimes he berated them from the pulpit, and ordered the men at the back to come forward and fill the front pews, and when they did, scolded the secrets they kept in their hearts. He arrived unannounced through the back doors of cottages. When he came to our house to visit the doctor, or to collect him for fishing, if he saw me he always said things such as, *Ah, here's the boss of the house himself!* or, *If I gave you a thru'penny bit, young man, would you know what to do with it?*

The river bend, glimpsed through trees, jumps alive as mist sighs from the hedgerows. Along the top of post-and-rails a grey squirrel scurries. Pigeon-song thrums in the morning glades. By the time I pull up by the bridge, sunlight is creeping into the sloping farmland, nailing tiny details, such as white stones in drainage gullies and pearls of moisture on the heads of daffodils. The stone-built, eighteenth-century residence seems far too near the road. A car is parked on one side of the porch, a large caravan on the other. As I step back to get a better view, I realize with shock why the proportions are so altered. The beech trees have gone. Hillocks, like graves, mark the stumps. The beech were planted the same year the house was built and what is left holds no meaning.

As I glide through a valley of dense trees, colours bright as coral glint. This is isolated country, far from the main road. In the old days the farmers up here seldom came to town. After the riverbed, a sharp climb leads to lush fields divided by grass-grown stone banks and home to speckled cattle. In a gateway, I get out and, looking back, cup my hands to my ears.

Moooooooaaaaaugh!

8

Jesus was everywhere: in a group of twice-life-size statues, depicting the Passion of Christ in Flannery's meadow, through which we had to drive, and, in a tiny figurine over every shed door lintel of the grey-painted farm outbuildings, as the Infant of Prague.

Father McVee always referred to him as Our Dear Lord, Jesus Christ. The priest had started dropping by our house on Sundays after Mass, and sat in the front room with the doctor, going through fishing books and magazines where the merits of sherry spinners, ginger quills and grey dusters were discussed. Colour paintings of the flies revealed themselves as the doctor, or the priest, carefully peeled back the protective tissue pages.

The fly-tier's art involves the hackles of game cocks, the feathers from duck wings and the stripped eye quills of peacocks.

No Flannery is listed in the telephone book for this area and at the shop where I stopped, they shook their heads. Have I really been here before, in this soft but remote landscape, this hidden parish of few homesteads so different from the sprawling expanses of Muskoka?

Twice I drive up and down the same stretch of narrow road before realising what has changed: in place of Flannery's old field gate, a bell-shaped entrance and modern concrete piers have been installed. An avenue divides the front field, and on either side of it stand rows of poplar, forty feet high. My rented car rattles on the cattle grid.

The sense of returning to a place I once knew is minimal. Water troughs and aluminium gates. A modern house with shiny slates and large windows is at odds with the old place, now revealed, hunched in beside the new. Concrete licks down from the house into the yard, like a dirty apron.

'Looking for someone?'

At my window stands a ginger-haired man who is no more than thirty, wearing a sleeveless singlet and shorts. He holds a pitchfork and his sweating body glistens.

9

'You stay in the car, mind,' said the doctor.

He sounded the horn, a few sharp pips, then got out. From a shed across the pockmarked dirt yard, frantic scuffling and barking erupted. The dwelling house, neatly thatched with little braids and twists of straw artfully woven above the eaves, glowed in the sunshine. I climbed into the driver's seat, its leather warm, clasped the steering wheel and imagined myself driving.

A man hurried towards us. Mr Flannery's hair was both black and white, like the coat of a badger, and from his chin sprouted a ragged black and white beard. Knitted mats of dark curls covered his thick forearms; damp patches marked the front of his flannel shirt.

'The fishing is mighty here these nights, Jim. Would you not take it up again?' the doctor asked as the farmer led the way to the house.

'I might, doctor, I might,' Mr Flannery replied, 'but I never seem to have the time.'

Fly fishing allows man to revert to his state of being a natural hunter and to stalk his quarry as he has done since memory began. Fly fishing allows man to act out an elemental part of the forest glade that lies within us all.

10

The farmer regards me with suspicion as he rests on his pitchfork, both hands on the shaft.

'Flannery,' he says and spits to the side. 'We found a prayer book inside in a box belonging to a Mrs Flannery. But this farm has changed hands three times since.'

The cottage door opens and a young woman comes out, looks at me, then picks up a pail and continues across the yard.

'They have a bench in the church,' he says. 'I think they're buried up there.'

'Just them? I mean, only the husband and wife?'

'The man you should talk to is Father Seán Phelan. Father Phelan knows everything.'

A wind is getting up, warm and laden with summer.

'No one ever came back here?' I ask. 'No one ever came in and said they'd lived here?'

'My wife is from this parish. Tess!'

Tess puts down the pail. She is pregnant and wears a cotton dress and shit-stained rubber boots to her bare knees.

'This man is asking about Flannerys that used to be here.'

'Oh, Flannerys,' she says and looks at me with curiosity. Her foxy hair is tied back tight from her freckled cheeks. 'Mr and Mrs Flannery.'

'I told him Father Phelan was his man.'

'Flannerys are buried beside the church,' she says.

'I told him that.'

I'm willing her to say more, for there is an instant quality of wisdom to Tess that is bewitching.

'I'm trying to contact a young boy who used to live here with them,' I say. 'His name was Terence.'

She screws up her face. 'When I was growing up, there used to be stories.' She glances at her husband. 'You know, stories.'

'There was trouble,' I say.

'Why the big interest?' the farmer asks.

'I live in Canada now. I'm trying to track down people I used to know here.'

'Flannery died, before her,' Tess says, 'and she left the farm to the parish priest. He sold the farm and used the money to rebuild the church.'

'What did Flannery die of, d'you know?'

She sees me only as an outsider.

'Don't ask me,' she says. 'It was a long time ago.'

11

Even though it was forbidden, I got out of the Humber. Timeless peace lay on the day, its drowsiness enlarging my senses as I walked across the yard, borne along by the droning of insects and the ripe scents of dung stacks and rich meadows.

By an old hay barn with open sides, I could see to the valley beyond. Pigeons flew out over my head in a tight covey. In the barn, shadows fell like broad planks as I walked through and out the other side to where a crab apple tree of small, stunted buds grew crookedly from a bank of earth. Thirty yards below, a boy was cranking the handle of a water pump. Brown legs, broad shoulders. Older than me, but not much. Black hair curled on his neck. The water bounced into the air like silver coins. He turned and saw me. He was frowning. *What is the matter with him?* was my first thought. *Why does he look so sad?*

Trout have spherical lenses that provide a wide field of vision. Their eyes can move independently of each other. They can see colours perfectly well, but since colours are not visible at night, a black fly is best for night fishing since it creates a clear silhouette against the moonlit sky.

12

Kay sits with a coffee, trying to read, listening to the east wind that sings in the roof. It's just gone eight-thirty and Keith has called from Roger's Quay, saying he'll be over in an hour. Tim appears at the door of the kitchen, looking bored.

'You want something to eat, Tim?'

'No, thanks, Grandma.'

'What do you want to do today?'

'Keith said he'd bring me water-skiing. Can I?'

'Not till Granddad comes home.'

'Please.'

'No. And that's the end of it. Look, why don't you go over and see what Pierre is up to?'

She watches fondly as the small figure makes his way out. She sees me as a small boy too, when it comes to my father, a child who must keep trying to be accepted, she will later say. My novel *Sulphur*, she understands, was another attempt to be accepted. The doctor of the book, a crusty old widower with a heart of gold, was hard on his only son, fearing that to indulge him would be to spoil him; and the son was often bewildered by his father's seeming rejection, and the beatings, losses of temper, and the bouts of lonely drunkenness. And yet the underlying love between the father in the book and his son was heart-warming, the emotions beautifully etched and delivered, Kay felt.

Sulphur did not tell the whole story, however, since it spoke only of one boy, whereas now it seems there were two. Death can mean so many different things, for the unconscious plays tricks, ever spinning its symbols, trying to make us confront the truth through our dreams. Dreams are seldom literal, Kay knows: her patients dream and then see conspiracies where there are none until their lives become ruined by suspicion.

Moreover, the doctor in the book was depicted as a good and noble man whose human failings were rescued by his honourable instincts. Was this the eulogizing to which I had referred and to which someone called Terence may have taken exception?

Kay puts down the magazine she has been reading, brings her fingertips to her temples and tries to press a little ease in there. Sometimes, as now, she says a quick prayer to make things right. The east wind sings. Soon it will go into the south and a new song will be heard in the roof tiles.

13

For decades I have lain awake in the Canadian vast-
ness imagining the landscape through which I am
now forging, seeing the roll of vernal hill fields,
hearing stream on stone, smelling sweet gorse. The
village, a small collection of buildings with the
church as its focal point, lies so hidden that one
always comes upon it with surprise. Uncountable
Sundays at Mass here with the doctor stand frozen
in my mind. He always timed it so that we arrived as
the Mass bell was pealing. Generations clung to the
forms and pews. In winter, the church was so cold
that the doctor unfailingly remarked, 'No wonder
there's so much chilblains.'

Sunlight pours down the empty main street. The
pub is still there, and so is the shop beside it, although
that has become a supermarket. Next is the church,
with its cemetery gathered tight around it. The church
door is closed, something that formerly would never
have been seen at noon. As I drive past, bells that are
not bells but electronic recordings burst from the bell-
tower. I remember Father McVee directing altar boys
to the rope of the old bell, a task seen as a reward for
diligence on the altar. Now each reverberating beat of

the midday Angelus, delivered in a fug of static, follows me out along the road.

The trout has inner ears, which allows him to distinguish sounds, particularly sounds too low for humans to hear. Lateral lines on either side of the trout's body transmit vibrations in the water to his brain. He uses this information to find food and to escape predators.

14

Pea gravel crunches on my approach to the hall door: dining room to the right, sitting room to the left; upstairs, three windows: the frosted panes of the bathroom and the two windows of the priest's bedroom. Do priests in Ireland still employ housekeepers, I wonder? Father McVee's, I suddenly recall, was called Miss McGinty.

A chain is undone and two locks turn.

'Father Phelan?'

He squints into the brightness. He is wearing a grey cardigan. His Roman collar is unclipped and hanging to one side of his shirt.

'Yes?'

'Seán, I'm Alex Smyth.'

Father Phelan runs his tongue back and forth along the inside of his lower lip, as if searching for food particles. In his mid-sixties, he is stooped and bald.

'Alex Smyth.'

'Do you remember me, Seán?'

All the decades rush into a single point in his pale blue eyes. 'You got married and...' He is confused. 'Where do you live?'

'In Canada.'

Trouble hatches in his suddenly anxious look. He

makes to step back inside.

'Alex, I'm sorry, but…'

'I just want to ask you something, that's all.'

'I have to go out shortly.'

'This will just take a minute.'

The priest sighs. 'You'd better come in so.'

Defiant fair curls still cluster on the back of his neck. A smell of stale drink. We turn left, to the sitting room, although from its coldness and bareness it is clear he has not been sitting here. A gilt-framed painting of the Sacred Heart hangs over the mantelpiece; beneath it is a dish containing an unlit night-light.

'Chain on the door these days, Seán. Two bolts.'

The priest offers up the palms of his hands.

'I have to take home the chalices after every Mass… Different times.' He goes to the window and drops the blind. 'It's hard to keep going.'

We sit on upright chairs.

'I saw my father yesterday.'

'When you say you saw him…?'

The priest's tone carries in it the possibility that what I've just referred to is a corpse.

'He's in a home outside Waterford, still to the good. Reads the paper. Still cantankerous.'

'Ah, thank God,' the priest says reflexively. 'I never knew him well, as you know, although I do know that he and my, ah, predecessor were acquainted.'

'He doesn't want to see me anymore.'

The tongue, like a sensor, moves beneath the lip. 'Well, there are consequences to everything.'

'I was in Flannery's old farm an hour ago.'

He blinks. 'Flannery's?'

81

'Flannerys that was.'

'Walshes have it now. That was parish land, you know.'

'Left to the Church by Flannerys.'

'Thomas and Agnes Flannery. Buried above. Let me see. He died in nineteen fifty-seven.' The priest is staring at me as if something unsavoury has just appeared. 'And his wife followed him in nineteen sixty-three, if I'm not mistaken,' he continues.

'And she was the sickly one.'

Father Phelan looks mildly surprised.

'She was my father's patient,' I explain.

'God be merciful to them both.'

Although caught off-guard by my arrival, now his attitude displays a mounting defiance.

'So what brought you out to Flannery's, Alex?'

'Trying to find out exactly what happened there.'

Father Phelan shakes his head. 'Before my time.'

'There was a boy called Terence. Something happened. What became of him?'

Father Phelan's eyes are empty. 'Terence?'

'Flannery's nephew. Come on, Seán!'

As if the utterance of a blatant lie is a step too far, he suddenly stands up.

'I think it is unfair to come in here like this, disturbing my morning, asking questions like a policeman.'

'Hardly.'

'Stirring it all up again... interfering.'

'Something is haunting me,' I say and my voice is unsteady. 'It has been with me all my life, but now it has come back with a vengeance.'

Father Phelan's forehead is a mosaic of bright pearls.

He shakes his head, as if he's had enough, but then he sits down again and says: 'Terence.'

'What was his second name?'

The priest frowns. 'Deasy. He was Mrs Flannery's nephew.'

'Terence Deasy.'

'All right? Now you have it.'

'I have another question—sorry, just hear me out—where is Terence now?'

'How the hell would I know? For Jesus' sake, I'm not the custodian of you and your family's friends!' he cries.

'Could he be in Canada? It's important, Seán.'

'I don't know.'

'So he could be?'

'I don't fucking know — all right?' The priest is trembling, whether from rage or fear. 'I'm sorry, Alex. You really need to direct your questions elsewhere. Now...' he looks at his watch.

'Tell me where to ask.'

He places his chin on the tips of his joined, upright fingers, as if composing himself. 'Charlie McVee went into Wilkins Abbey.'

'When?'

'When... everything came out. You know.'

'I went to Canada over forty years ago.'

'Wilkins were the only people who'd take him in.'

'Did you ever visit him?'

'Me? Jesus, no! I had nothing to do with him, ever. No one went near him. No one even went to the funeral.' Father Phelan once more checks his watch. 'I told you, I have to be somewhere.'

'I'm going.'

He opens his front door and sunlight streams in. On the road below, two boys spin by on bicycles.

He says, 'He was befriended by one or two of the monks up there. Maybe they'll know what you want.'

'I'm sorry to have intruded.'

He lets out a long sigh and I smell the stale alcohol again.

'Do you know what it's like for us nowadays? Those of us who stayed the course?' he asks.

'You don't have to justify yourself to me.'

'We're marked men. I can see it in their eyes at Mass. Oh, sure, they defer to my office when it suits them, but deep down they despise me and what I represent. We're finished here. Finished.'

'I'm very sorry.'

He lowers his gaze. Eyelashes still fair, as I remember them.

'We've known each other for a long time,' he says. 'Since we went to school together. And after.'

'I know.'

'We had some good times,' he says and all at once smiles.

A bubbling ten-year-old with a shock of fair curly hair. A crucifix in his hands, dressed in a snowy white alb, preceding Father McVee from the altar to the sacristy.

His smile becomes sad. 'You and me, we once... You see, I only ever tried to do what I thought was best.'

Life is so strange, I think, and so cruel.

'Seán, if you're ever in Canada...' I say, handing him the card we had printed when we moved to Muskoka.

'I'll pray for you,' Father Phelan says and closes his door.

15

The trout has a powerful ability to smell, which is difficult for humans to understand, since smelling underwater is a faculty we lack. When a sea trout becomes sexually mature, perhaps after one or more summers in the ocean, he turns homewards to his childhood river to breed, directed unerringly and entirely by his sense of smell.

Kay is baking. The electric mixer is churning, a baking tray lined with buttered, grease-proof paper lies awaiting its contents and the oven. With the big kitchen scissors she shreds tiny pieces of lemon zest into the mixture. From overhead comes gentle tapping as Keith re-beds the shingles and re-fixes them to the cross-beams with the brads he brought over from Roger's Quay. Out of the window, she can see where Tim is dragging a plastic goalmouth across the grass. The goal contraption is three times as large as he is.

Despite what she said on the phone about being fine, Kay finds Keith's presence comforting, she will say later; with Keith's pick-up parked out front, Larry is less likely to drop by. She has decided not to think about Larry, or of who he may really be, or if he is in fact stalking her. She has also decided to stay at home until I get back, because if she goes into Bayport she may bump into Larry. Nor is she going over to the hospital until next week: she's called in and cancelled her appointments.

She's safe here in our home, in the midst of domestic activity. And maybe all this commotion—which is probably no more than coincidence—is for the best. The rift with my father was never resolved, and sometimes Kay thinks that this was because of her. Had I been alone, without having to consider her feelings, I might have laid the groundwork for reconciliation, however difficult. Now my trip to Ireland may somehow bring everyone together.

The image at her office window that night in Charlton suddenly pops up and she shudders. Yesterday, she called the hospital and spoke to a person she knows in admissions. Larry said he was visiting a friend on the night in question, but now Kay has learned that there were no in-patients in the hospital that night whose name she recognizes. It doesn't mean that Larry can't have friends she doesn't know... but still.

She knocks off the mixer, dislodges the bowl, takes a wooden spoon and begins to scoop out the mixture into the baking tray. Kay pauses and listens. The metronomic tapping from the roof has ceased.

'Keith?'

She knows he can hear her because she called him down earlier for coffee. Outside, through the window, the empty lawn lies in sudden shadow. Still grasping the wooden spoon and mixing bowl, she steps out to the porch.

'Keith! Tim!'

She puts down the bowl and begins to walk quickly. The emptiness is all at once overpowering. Kay forces herself not to run across the path that leads to the front gate, then without warning, she is transfixed by sunlight. In the bright space that separates our house from the Echenozs', Keith is in goal, Tim is about to kick.

16

The panorama plunges into valleys of purple-flowering rhododendron intersected by silver streams. In one direction the distant sea is at once infinite and comforting, and in the other, on the crest of a ridge to the north-west, a row of jagged crenellations appears. As a child, I came up here twice a year with the doctor: at Easter and at Christmas, when he made his confession. What sins lay deep in the doctor's heart? What whispered words could be spoken only to a monk in this cloistered fortress?

For the final mile, the road climbs at a steep angle. Lone trees, cleft by lightning, clutch to rock. The sense of desolation I once felt returns as I drive under the stone arch. When a man dies in here, the doctor used to say, all his possessions fit into a shoebox.

A door, tucked beneath an old masonry buttress, opens into a small office where a white-robed monk sits at a computer.

'The lawnmower,' he says to me.

His skin glows, his head is shaven.

'The lawnmower,' he says again. 'Am I right?'

No eyebrows, prominent cheekbones and discoloured teeth. I have no idea how old he is.

'Afraid not, Father.'

'Brother. Brother Malachy. But as Saint Augustine said, a thing is not necessarily false because badly uttered, nor true because spoken magnificently. How can I help you?'

'Alex Smyth. I live in Canada.'

'Ah! How I often dream of it, although I've never been there. And yet I detect a slight Irish accent.'

'My father used to come here to have his confession heard.'

'In the days no doubt when that holy sacrament was more widely availed of. And did you not confess yourself, Alex?'

'I was a child.'

'I still remember my first confession,' he says thoughtfully. 'Tongue-tied I was. The poor man on the other side of the grille had to come around and see if there was someone in there at all.'

An elfin quality attaches to this monk of indeterminate age whose robes rustle as he leans back in the chair, hands behind his head.

'And is it confession you're after today, Alex? If I can find you a priest, that is. I'd be off down the fields myself if I wasn't on duty.'

'I need some information, about a resident of the abbey, now deceased.'

'Oh, well, in that case the abbot is your man, but he's in Rome, I'm afraid.'

'The priest I'm referring to is Father Charles McVee.'

The monk's slow nod. 'I see. I see.'

'I understand he died here.'

'Indeed he did.'

'Did you know him, Brother Malachy?'

Brother Malachy's expression is a mixture of wariness and provisional affirmation. 'Long time ago.'

'That's what everyone says.'

'And yet it is incontestably true.'

I have to smile. 'When did he die?'

'When did Charlie die? Let me see. How old am I?' He goes through some form of personal calculation. 'Twelve years ago? Maybe fourteen.'

'So you remember him.'

'I may do – but why?' Brother Malachy cocks his head like a bird listening for a worm.

'I find this very hard to talk about, because I am ashamed and afraid, and because it is caught somewhere inside me and I don't know what it is or how to get it out.'

The monk exhales in a slow whistle of air.

'What was your father's name?'

'Paddy Smyth. Doctor Paddy Smyth. He's still alive.'

Brother Malachy gets to his feet, his garments cumbersome in the small space, and locks his desk, using keys from a bunch on his leather belt.

'If you'd like to follow me, please, Alex.'

17

The trout is a beautiful creature. His colouring is the most delicate brushwork on a glistening sheen, exquisitely streamlined: now gold and olive, now blue and silver, now mottled with spots red and black.

As Brother Malachy walks between squarely built stone fortifications, the soles of his sandals slap evenly against his heels. Near the door to the church, where a boarded-up souvenir shop makes up one half of a prefabricated wooden building, he again fingers out a key, unlocks the door beside the shop, turns on the light and plugs in an electric kettle.

'My canteen.'

He sets out two cups, milk and sugar, then goes about making tea. At a plain table, he stirs the pot, but resists the urge to pour, as if all impulses have to be restrained.

'I never met your father, but I know who he is.'

'May I ask how?'

He looks to the window, the church, the slopes of the mountain, the other world.

'I was twenty-one years of age when I came in here. I had a degree in history and originally thought I was going to be a teacher. But then my vocation swept me up and carried me away. I fell in love.'

He dwells for a sweet moment, like a bride who has come across her wedding photographs.

'The then abbot did his best to talk me out of it, but I wouldn't budge. Everything will have to be left behind, including your transistor radio, he told me. Neither could I have visitors, nor ever leave. Fine, I told him, that is what I want. So he put me in charge of Charlie McVee.'

'In charge?'

'A way of testing me, I suppose. Charlie was prematurely old, sick, mostly incontinent. His chest was very bad and we had not yet got the heating in. Although it was quite obvious he hadn't long to live, he'd already died many times. I'm talking about a wreck of a human being. His priestly faculties had been removed by Rome. He was an outcast. If he hadn't been taken in here, he would have perished on the side of the road.'

Brother Malachy pours out two cups of tea. He takes two sugar cubes in his.

'I remember him as a big, brazen man,' I say.

'Interesting, because although he was never big when I knew him, he was still brazen.'

'In what way?'

'His attitude.'

'Did he talk to you?'

'Oh, yes. Every day. I can still hear Charlie talking.'

18

A trout that has come home to breed becomes increasingly aggressive as his sexual nature takes over. Even if driven from his lie by predators, he will return as quickly as he can when the danger has passed.

One morning I heard the doctor remark to Mrs Tyrrell, 'Father McVee is keeping an eye on that situation in Flannery's.'

'God bless Father McVee,' replied Mrs Tyrrell, ever ready to display her devotion to the curate.

'That boy has come through hell,' the doctor said. 'He may need professional care.'

I had not heard the doctor refer to the boy in Flannery's before and this mention of him seemed like an intrusion into what I had come to consider as my secret. The boy had looked like Man Friday in my *Robinson Crusoe*, a wild figure with bare, exotic skin. As I lay in bed, I imagined myself sleeping on an island beach with him, the dark sea lapping, the moon licking our legs.

When the doctor was called upon by a patient in Waterford the following evening, a visit that would take more than two hours, Mrs Tyrrell bathed me, a practice that had evolved over the years in the doctor's absence.

'How are we going to get a bit of fat on you at all, Alex? Seven years of age and you're still like a lat'.'

As Mrs Tyrrell's motherly hands guided soapy water over my limbs, I was seized without warning by a feeling of intense longing. Images jumped at me. I felt myself swell and grow deliciously outside my control as she soaped my thighs. Mrs Tyrrell, suddenly seeing what was happening, stood up abruptly and went over to the far side of the bathroom to dry her hands.

'Mrs Tyrrell?'

'Yes, child?'

'What is that situation in Flannery's?'

'Oh ho! Ears on bushes!'

'It's that boy, isn't it?'

'You say your prayers that you are where you are and not where that poor boy is,' she said, carrying over a large bath towel which she kept held out between us. 'A drunkard for a father, the farm gone and the mother in an early grave, God help her. Say your prayers, Alex Smyth.'

19

The larger caddis flies, also called sedges or flags, have a tendency to start hatching at dusk, and on calm, warm evenings this can go on long into the night. They begin life under water as larvae, a phase that lasts for around ten months. Inside a sac spun from its own intestines, the larva metamorphoses into a pupa, before biting its way out into the world. The black-headed insect that emerges into the air has two pairs of wings and its long antennae can be twice its body length.

The all-purpose fly designed to mimic this insect, and often used on moonlit nights, is called the coachman.

For weeks the doctor had been talking about the medical conference in Dublin. Colleagues from his old university days, and from England, even a professor from the United States of America would gather in the Gresham Hotel. I came to know all the details: how he would drive to Kilkenny and catch the Dublin train; then in Dublin hail a taxi-cab to take him from the station to the hotel, where a room had been reserved; and how, before retiring, if you put your shoes outside your bedroom door, you would find them shining clean next morning. Mrs Tyrrell would stay the night in our house, something so unheard of that it made me sick with excitement. But with twenty-four hours to go, Mrs Tyrrell went down with flu and so it was hastily arranged that I stay with Father McVee.

'His housekeeper, Miss McGinty, is a very fine woman, just like Mrs Tyrrell,' the doctor said.

I must have shown my disappointment.

'And,' the doctor allowed a little smile to tug at his moustache, 'he says he might even take you fishing.'

We got up at seven and the doctor fried trout with tomatoes. We ate together for the first time ever in the kitchen. The doctor then brought out a small leather suitcase that had once belonged to my mother.

'The last time I saw this was after the honeymoon,' he said as I took it from him and went upstairs to pack my things.

I loved my father more than ever then, for I knew this suitcase represented his lost life. I could imagine my mother unpacking the clothes she had worn in the west of Ireland, where they had spent ten days after their marriage: removing her formal dresses and shoes, gloves and blouses, all of which still hung or lay in her wardrobe, where I sometimes went to plunge my face in the faintly lingering scents that still attached to the fabrics: then her calling down 'Paddy, can you take this case?' And the doctor, not realising that within thirty-six months he would never again be called Paddy in that house, would have come up the stairs. Did they kiss at that moment, I wondered? They both smiled, I was sure, the way they were smiling in photographs. When Paddy closed the empty case and lifted it from their bed, did he ever imagine in a thousand dreams that his wife would never see that suitcase again? It would probably have been better, I reasoned, if both of them had died then.

We loaded up the car just after eight and set out through the rolling hills where a stranger could never suspect a village might exist. All at once, in the tributary valley that made the surrounding farmland so rich, there it was, its church spire proudly fixing the community to its place.

The parish priest's house, separated from the road by a garden of sweet pea and roses, had been built, as the doctor had once explained, following the granting of Catholic Emancipation in 1829. Holding my hand, he carried my suitcase in over the crunchy gravel. Suddenly I remembered Father McVee at Sunday Mass, his booming voice ordering men up from the back of the church.

I pulled back. 'I want to go home.'

'Alex...'

'I don't want to stay here. I want to go home!'

My sudden aversion momentarily outweighed my fear of the doctor's disapproval. Something extraordinary then took place. My father squatted down to be level with me, and in a soft, conciliatory voice said, 'Be a good little boy, now, please. The doctor doesn't get away very often, does he? And think of how disappointed Father McVee will be. He's looking forward to bringing you fishing.'

As my tears came silently and quickly, the doctor took out a red spotted handkerchief and patted my cheeks.

'Do you know something? You look the living image of your poor mam. She'll never be dead for me as long as you're here.'

He had never before said anything like that and I recognized how his words reflected the desperation of the situation. Then the hall door opened and Father McVee appeared in a regimental black soutane, gleaming black brogues and a broad Roman collar. He came towards me, his arms flapping.

'Well, well, well,' he said.

'I'm delivering your lodger, father,' the doctor said, getting back to his feet. 'It's his first time.'

'Miss McGinty has made the biggest pot of porridge I've ever seen in my life,' said Father McVee happily.

20

Whatever kind of water he inhabits, the trout is an expert at survival: in knowing where the food is, and how to get it, and, when he is not feeding, in conserving his energies and keeping out of trouble. He soon discovers that tiny, vulnerable creatures like flies and nymphs are at the mercy of the currents, so, not unnaturally, he positions himself to take advantage of the flows.

In the sitting room, I listened to the big, mahogany-encased wireless, and spun the dial between Hilversum and Berlin, Stockholm and Athlone, as I did at home. Father McVee had driven to Clonmel, to visit the industrial school, following which he would return to the village to hear confessions, Miss McGinty told me.

As each hour passed, I tried to imagine the doctor's progress: on the train, off the train, in his hotel arranging to be called in time for his conference in the morning. I wandered in and out of the kitchen, where the house-keeper was preparing dinner; but she lacked the spontaneous affection of Mrs Tyrrell and seemed uncomfortable to have a child interrupting her solitary routines.

Father McVee poured himself a glass of sherry, sat at the head of his dining room table and peered down at me. Outside, over the garden, dusk spread like black dye.

'It's not often I have a visitor.'

Miss McGinty carried in a soup tureen, set it down and began to ladle out.

'Our guest,' the priest indicated when she tried to place a soup plate in front of him. 'By the look of the creature, he needs it more than I do.'

Soup of any kind was not to my liking, a fact that influenced Mrs Tyrrell when designing her menus.

'I'd say by the smell that you've excelled yourself, Miss McGinty. What is it at all?'

'Legumes, father.'

'Legumes, by golly,' he remarked, in a voice that reminded me of a hooting owl.

When Miss McGinty had left, he tipped what was left of his sherry into the soup plate. As I dragged my spoon around, causing unnamed vegetables to break the surface, I could feel the weight of the priest's gaze. Once, when I glanced up, I saw he wasn't eating, but staring at me, open-mouthed. At one point, he went to the sideboard and refilled his glass. Nose to my plate, I pretended to be eating, but knew that he was still staring.

'We'll try Flannery's for trout later. Would you like that, Master Smyth?'

'Yes, please, Father.'

He made a low throaty sound. 'Oh, be the boys, be the boys! Ah, yes! Oh, be the boys.'

21

'He underwent a number of psychiatric examinations. In hospital they put machines on his head, then showed him the pictures. "You have a psychological disorder", they told him. He never disagreed. "Why did you decide to become a priest?" they asked him. "It was always decided", he said. "You mean", they said, "you did not decide yourself—is that what you mean, Charlie?" "What I mean is", he said, "that my mother decided." The doctors looked at their files. "But your mother was dead, Charlie", they told him, "she died when you were born",' Brother Malachy says.

22

We climbed from the village and the headlights of the priest's Morris Minor picked out the white-tipped brush of a fox stepping watchfully along the hedgerow. Across the back seat lay fishing rods in canvas sleeves. The warm evening was intermittently bathed by a moon in its final quarter.

More than once I had had to look to confirm that the man at the wheel, dressed in an open-necked checked shirt and corduroys, really was Father McVee. At Flannery's road gates, he sat there expectantly.

'Well come on, young lad, hop out!'

I hauled back the heavy gates with difficulty, waited until the car came bumping through, then dragged them closed again.

'You're a weak little eel, aren't you?' he said as I got back in.

Our lights soon picked out the crooked whitethorns with their religious ornaments and the clean outlines of the farm buildings. Darkness enclosed us. As the dog in the shed began to snarl and bark, I expected to see Mr Flannery hurrying out, as he always did, an air of distraction about him. Instead, the priest sounded the horn. His breath whistled and he drummed the steering wheel with his fingers. He sounded the horn again. I could see high shadows moving within the house and realized that Flannery's still used oil lamps. Dim light cracked the jamb of the door.

Trout fishing is the most elegant of ballets: the man with only the rod in his hand, his prey a thing of silver beauty in the water, the line of communication between man and fish as delicate as gossamer.

'Push over, Master Smyth, and let him in there beside you.'

I felt a jolt to my hip as I was pushed in across the seat. The priest turned the car and we headed back for the road.

'Are you all right tonight, laddie?'

I glanced over and saw the boy looking ahead, his left arm braced against the dashboard. The sadness that I had noticed on the first day still clung to his expression. As we drew near the road, he jumped out and the headlights pinned him as he lifted back the gates.

'You see how lovely and strong Terence is?' the priest said. 'We'll have to make you big and strong like that, Master Smyth.'

To get at Flannery's stretch of river, you had to drive downhill on the road and then re-enter the bottom portion of the farm through a series of level fields. The priest hummed happily as the last slice of the moon occasionally flashed through high cloud and sparked off moving water. By a gatepost, we parked.

'Terence has the boots on already. He knows the routine down here, don't you, Terence?'

The priest slipped out the component parts of the split-cane rod and fitted them together, his hands sure. He took out a reel, threaded the silk line through the eyelets, and then, using the lights of the car, chose a black-headed fly from a box, tied it fast to catgut, joined it to the silk line, made the knot neat with a pair of scissors, hauled the dressed line through and snagged the hook on to the cork rod handle.

'This lad is called the coachman, Master Smyth. He's your only man at night.'

As he shook out a second rod, I looked for Terence. The headlights made a wall of blackness. Hand to my eyes, I walked around the car and waited until the glare ebbed from my vision. He was sitting on the ground by the rear wheel, arms around his knees, head forward so that all I could see was his hair.

'Terence?'

He didn't move.

'Terence, have you ever caught a trout?'

I got down beside him, edging in close until my back was also to the wheel.

'I like being down here,' I whispered as bands of pale moonlight drifted across us.

Slowly his face appeared. He looked at me through slits and along his row of upper teeth were black gaps. I thought he was going to tell me something, but he tilted back his head, gathered saliva in his mouth, and spat at me.

'What are you wee lads up to?'

Father McVee's head came into view.

'Nothing, Father,' Terence mumbled.

'Now,' the priest said, handing a rod to him, 'Master Smyth will carry the baskets, please.'

Single file, the priest to the fore, we walked through a narrow gap and into ferns that came to my chest. Clouds hurried over the dying moon. I was mystified that Terence didn't like me, for I had never done anything to him; and yet, when he had spat at me, he had been filled with venom. Nonetheless, I wanted to be near him. He walked ahead of me on ground that fell away to the river. A hunting bird screeched as it rose before us. Fast-flowing water could suddenly be heard.

'This is where we start from and where you stay,' the priest whispered, taking the baskets from me and placing them on the ground, ten paces from the river. 'There's an apple in there, for being a good wee lad.'

Immediately he began to cast out into the mid-stream where no trees overhung. I could not see the far bank. Terence was twenty yards farther along, casting, the rod light in his hands. A trout slurped. Weak moonbeam showed a midge hatch for an instant, a fuzz above the water. I looked to where Terence, moving along, had all but disappeared. The priest followed him.

23

Time that evening is difficult for me to measure. Although thrilled by darkness and the presence of the unknown, I was gripped too by a sense of unspecified danger. I felt insects on my neck and legs. Now and then a fish broke upwards and sipped; and once, at the exact moment when the last of the moon lay in a narrow track on the water, a brown trout made a spectacular leap, and hung for a beautiful shining instant, impaled on the shaft of light, water drawn up from his tail in a moon-silver skirt. I wondered if I should call to the others that fish were rising here, but the imperative of silence had been hammered into me by my father. As I searched for movement in the reeds and the shadows, there was a cry. A man's long cry that split the night. Ah! They've caught one, I thought!

The young trout that lies in shallow waters leads a dangerous existence, and not always a long one, since he is easily visible to predators. The older trout leads a very different life. He feeds in slower and deeper waters. No darting this way and that for him, no extrovert or suicidal lunges. He has all the time in the world

to scrutinize his prey. Seldom will he emerge into the
shallows, unless the urge to mate takes its hold.

'My father came back from Dublin the next day, and
I went home.'

'Did you understand what had happened?'

'My reflex answer is, no—how could I have? I was
a gormless seven-year-old kid. But on another level,
which I suppose was my sexual level, something was
stirring. Chemistry. I think in my bones I knew what
had happened, but my brain could not imagine it.'

24

The doctor had purchased a car radio in Dublin and had it tuned most of the day to Athlone. As we met the hills and dips of south Tipperary, he turned down the volume and began to chat about the conference in Dublin, where he had met colleagues and had been invigorated by the papers presented by consultants from overseas.

I thought endlessly of Terence and of how I wanted to be like him—to know how to cast and be able to so easily lift back a gate. A week passed and then, late one afternoon, when the schools had closed for the summer, we were stopped by a flag in the window of a house beyond Carrick. Mrs Flannery's chest had relapsed.

'Why do these bloody people leave it till teatime to make the call?' the doctor cried as he turned east and my blood quickened.

The trout is like poetry as he throbs on the current, as the water slicks by his glistening form. He hypnotizes the eye with a magic that draws men down into a silent void, into a mysterious liquid womb.

'I'll be as quick as I can. Stay in the car.'

As the dog's barking ceased, the blossom of the

countryside folded over the earth. When I rolled down the window, I could smell dung smells, mingled with hen smells and the other dry, brittle scents of midsummer. The need to see Terence again twisted upwards in me. Inside the open door of a nearby shed hung black rubber thigh-waders. Hidden bantams chuckled in rafters. I stepped into the yard, and then ran for the barn, just as Terence walked out.

We stood there, staring at each other. A head taller than me and twice as broad, beneath his black hair his eyes stood out like seashells.

'What are you doing here?'

'Daddy...'

'Daddy the doctor! Daddy the doctor!' he sneered and I thought he was going to spit at me again. He looked at the Humber. 'Daddy's car.'

'It's a Humber Hawk.'

He said nothing.

'It's got optional overdrive and a radio,' I said. 'We can listen to Athlone.'

'Daddy the doctor!' he said mockingly and turned back into the barn.

I was used to being picked on in school, but Terence's disrespectful attitude to the doctor stunned me, since everyone knew the esteem in which my father was held in three counties. Still caught up in a surge of unexplained longing, I followed Terence inside to where a calf was penned. He must have been feeding the animal, for he swung his leg over the waist-high, horizontal poles and picked up a bottle. The white-snouted calf sucked hungrily on the rubber teat, ears flattened. 'Why do you have to feed it?'

He mustn't have heard me, I thought.

'Terence, why are you feeding it?'

He looked at me. 'Daddy the doctor's little boy!'

I looked in awe as he spat on the ground.

'His stupid mother died.'

It took me a moment to work out to what he was referring.

'My mother died,' I blurted.

The bottle whistled as the calf sucked it dry.

'She contracted septicaemia.'

He squinted out at me. 'What?'

'Blood poisoning. Daddy says it's a very painful death.'

'Think I care?'

'It took her three weeks to die.'

'I don't care if she died twenty times over. I don't care if she's in hell.'

'She may be in purgatory, Daddy says, but he's more certain that she's in heaven.'

'You're a real daddy's boy, aren't you?'

'My mother was a daily communicant. She said the rosary every night and she did the nine first Fridays. Anyone who does the nine first Fridays is guaranteed a place in heaven.'

Then I thought of Mrs Tyrrell's remarks.

'And *your* mother died,' I said.

He dropped the bottle and vaulted out. He caught me by the neck and pushed my face down until it was pressed into farm shit.

'Who said you could talk about my mother?'

The weight on my neck was unforgiving.

'No one.'

He shook me. 'Talk about her again and I'll kill you.'

As he let me go, I fell to one side and spat muck. He was leaning on the side of the pen, his gaze to the south, over the placid hills. I got up and wiped myself with straw. My legs and shoes were smeared with dung. I felt powerless in his company, weak and subjugated. He was so strong and confident, so abounding in all the qualities I lacked.

'Where do you live?' he asked me suddenly.

'With my father.'

'With Daddy the doctor. I know. But where?'

'Outside Carrick. On the Waterford road.'

He turned slowly and looked towards the car.

'I need to get to Waterford before anyone here knows I'm gone,' he said.

He went to the house side of the barn and looked at the Humber, then came back again.

'It's too far to walk without being caught.' When he spoke, I could see where his teeth were missing. 'Can you keep your mouth shut?'

I nodded, terrified.

'I'm going to Waterford.'

'Why?'

'When I sail to America.'

The pages of *Robinson Crusoe* swam before me.

'First the boats go to England, then to America,' he said. 'They're always looking for deckhands. America is a huge place. No one knows anyone there.'

I wiped myself with my sleeve. 'Have you told your uncle?'

He shook his head. 'Little fool.' He looked at me curiously. 'I'll go with you as far as Carrick.'

111

My mouth stung and I stank of shit, but a shaft of excitement tingled in me.

'I'll hide in the boot,' he said.

'The boot is full of medicines.'

'Then I'll hide in the back.'

I gawked at him, at his tanned skin and his long-fingered hands.

'Come here,' he said.

He reached into a barrel of water, slopped my face and rubbed the shit off.

'No one will know. Just you and me.'

Like a gunshot, the noise of the opening cottage door broke through the afternoon.

'Next time!' he whispered. 'When he comes back to see the aunt.'

I dashed through the barn and regained the back seat, just as the doctor appeared with Mr Flannery, the farmer anxious as usual.

'I don't know, dammit!' the doctor cried and Flannery rocked back. 'Just keep her on the balsam. I'll be back in a week.'

He slammed the car door and started the engine. His nostrils twitched.

'You were out of the car, weren't you?'

'No, Daddy. I was here the whole time.'

'Liar! Your shoes stink of manure. Take 'em off!'

'I needed to pee,' I whined.

'A liar is a bad trait,' the doctor said grimly as he drove over the field at greater speed than normal. 'A liar is like a corpse with worms in his belly—rotten inside—so you'd better get those worms out, young fella, or you'll have me to deal with.'

In his temper, he flung the car sideways and my head knocked off the walnut trim. As I scrambled to my knees, I saw the doctor's angry little eyes in the rear-view mirror.

'Know what I mean?'

25

'I asked him several times if he regretted what he had done,' Brother Malachy says. 'His answer was always the same. "Regret who I am? My nature? My instinct? Is my instinct wrong, that which God gave me? It may not be appropriate, or desirable in the wider sense, but it is me," he always said. On one occasion he described it as a flowering. The flower doesn't become transformed, he said; it just does what flowers do. It opens its lips and becomes filled with the essence necessary for its existence. That's what he told me.'

In those hazy days of late summer, when the morning mists lifted from the valleys of south Tipperary to reveal diamond-bright kingfishers hunting the banks of the Suir, and when, in the full heat of midday, hawks quivered in the white-blue sky, it seemed to me that my life was suspended. I had come to love and loathe the doctor, a contradiction that would endure into my adulthood. He could easily have specialized in a single branch of medicine and become a consultant in one of the large hospitals in Dublin or Cork, but that would have meant a different kind of life and the doctor was a countryman. And yet his self-imposed isolation and disappointment with life was becoming ever more apparent: the despondent stares at night; the intense feeling, articulated after whiskey, that his life could have amounted to more than this; and the sense conveyed, however obliquely, that I was largely to blame for his predicament.

I decided to run away with Terence. The thought tantalized me to the point of madness. I would bargain his place in our car for his agreement to take me with him. Images of a world without the doctor thrilled me. What lay ahead sucked me in and created a new need, which, although I scarcely knew it at the time, was the need to love someone other than the doctor.

26

When the trout takes a fly, he knows with the wisdom of generations that he is fighting for his life. His instinct, which just a moment before was contemplating the taste of a juicy spinner, has now switched to survival. Bursting through the crust of the water, like splintering glass, he shows himself in all his elemental and outraged beauty. His endgame has begun.

The good weather had lasted. As we nosed in across Flannery's pastures, a warm peace caressed the land. I was sick with apprehension and had lain awake for most of the nights before, fretting about what would happen if we were caught. My father's anger petrified me, the thought that he might find out what I had planned. I clung to the image of Terence's superior strength and knowledge that would spring us both from the worlds we hated. Inchoate images of America, picked up from cowboy comics, spun in my head.

As if the gaze of each Infant of Prague contained the knowledge of my secret, I prayed that the doctor would not look at the statues and realise the truth. The shed door in Flannery's yard was open and the thigh-waders visible, suspended as if a man were strung up in the void above them. The doctor pocketed his pipe, got out and tapped on the rear door window.

'Are you feeling out of sorts, lad?'

For want of a reply, I nodded. His attitude took on a professional slant.

'I might have known. It's this damn flu that's going. You need a hot drink and bed. Poor lad.'

'Doctor Smyth, thanks be to God!' cried Flannery from his front door. 'She's fit to burst!'

'I won't be long,' the doctor told me. 'Stay in the car.'

What was about to take place had filled my mind so completely that no room existed to work around it. I was too terrified to get out, terrified that Terence would appear, terrified that he wouldn't. The locked-up dog, tormented as ever by unseen intruders, scratched and snarled. Inside the barn, young cattle were gathered. Then I saw him.

A hundred times I had thought of this moment, but had not expected it to unfold so quickly. He came crouching from the barn, opened the back door of the Humber and slid in behind the driver's seat like a fox sliding into an earth.

'Shut the door!'

I could neither breathe nor hear. He was clutching a bulging jute sack, his travel belongings, a detail I had overlooked.

'The blanket,' he said.

'What?'

'The blanket. Cover me with the blanket!'

I instantly forgot the bargain I had planned to strike and threw the travelling rug over him. All became quiet and deathly still. Then a strong odour of stale milk and cow byre began to fill the car. Overcome by my memory of the last time, and the doctor's reaction, all my plans disappeared in a moment governed only by fear. I snatched away the rug.

'You have to get out. Quick!'

He bared his uneven teeth.

'Get out!'

If he had got out then, the future might have unfolded differently, but he grabbed back the rug with both hands. I wanted to vomit for fear.

'Get out!'

His mouth opened in a silent howl as he held the rug around him like a shawl. Suddenly he was no longer Man Friday, or strong and confident, but a frightened child with missing teeth.

'Get out!' I cried.

He looked up at me, his expression pitiable. Miserably trapped between my obligations to unnamed forces, I began to bawl.

'Get out. Get out! *Get out!*'

'I don't want to go fishing with him anymore.'

I may have fainted in that tiny moment of revelation; I may have sat back, as my head swam, I cannot say, for I was along by the river again in that fathomless black place that had once stood between my innocence and the rest of my life. Suddenly I understood more than I ever wanted to. The voice of the farmer's wife could now be heard, saying loudly, 'I promise I'll take it easy, doctor. You have my word.'

All I could think of was the doctor's reaction if he ever found out what this boy might reveal about his friend the priest. The rug in the foot well rose and fell gently. As the doctor and Mr Flannery walked across the yard, the doctor was saying, 'Fishing's good at the moment, Jim.'

'The very best, doctor.'

'Father McVee told me he killed a two-and-a-half pounder the other night.'

'Father McVee knows where they're hiding; no doubt at all about that.'

I heard their voices as if from under water.

'And this is the little lad,' smiled Mr Flannery and he knocked on the back window.

'Roll down the window, Alex.'

I did as I was told.

'What do you say to Mr Flannery, Alex?'

'How... how do you do, Mr Flannery,' I stammered as my ears roared.

'He's definitely coming down with something,' the doctor said grimly. 'Look at him, pale as a ghost. Come on, Alex, we'll get you home, boy.'

He got in and started the engine. Outside, Mr Flannery stood, concerned and grateful. As the doctor slipped the handbrake and we began to leave the yard, I experienced an instant of time suspended, in which I grasped, if only dimly, how the years ahead would be touched by this moment and how I lacked the strength to alter what was about to happen. We had entered the field where Christ's Passion stood graphically in the corner.

'Daddy?'

The doctor looked quizzically in his rear-view mirror.

'You know that boy who lives here?'

'The boy? What about him?'

'He's hiding in our car.'

The car bumped along for a few yards more, prolonging the suspension of time, as the doctor tried to make sense of what he had heard. He pulled up.

'*What?*'

'He's here, Daddy. Look.'

I pulled off the rug as the doctor squirmed around and stared down into the foot well.

'He made me let him hide,' I cried. 'He made me!'

'Lord God Almighty, help us and save us,' the doctor exclaimed. 'So he did, the little wretch!'

Terence began to weep and shiver. The doctor, unable for once to speak, shook his head. I withdrew into the far corner of the back seat, as if to escape contagion.

'What on earth's he doing in here?'

'Running away,' I sobbed.

'Why?'

'I don't know... he wouldn't tell me,' I said and began to cry in earnest.

'Dear Lord,' the doctor said as he wrenched around the wheel. 'Dear Lord.'

As we re-approached the farmyard, I resumed my long-time position on the back seat, looking out the window. If I tried hard, I could imagine that everything was as it had been: horses in the nearby field, their long wide backs gleaming with healthy condition; cattle munching in hock-high meadows; statues. Our arrival in the yard coincided with Mr Flannery's releasing of the imprisoned dog, a sly-looking, yellow-eyed creature that ran up to the car and began to bite frantically at the wheels. It took the farmer more than a minute to catch the animal and lock it away. The doctor climbed out and took Mr Flannery to one side. I couldn't turn around. The car's back door was opened.

'Terence?' Mr Flannery said.

My mother would save me, I knew, as I began to pray to her.

'God, doctor, I don't know what to say,' Mr Flannery said.

'This is a serious matter.'

'I know, but he's a good boy normally. He's had a hard time. His mammy died and you know the history there. Maybe we're too old for him here; maybe…'

As we pulled away again, as Terence stood beside Mr Flannery, clutching his jute sack, I felt immeasurable relief. My gaze through the back window of the car was fastened on the shed with the open door, where the black thigh-waders hung, heels kicking gently in the breeze.

27

Studying the stomach contents of trout between April and September will generally reveal a preference for sedge flies, midges and shrimps. In season, mayfly predominates, while other key foods are beetles, fish fry, snails and newts. In the winter, frogs become more important, as does the water louse.

In turn, trout are preyed upon by pike, herons, cormorants, gulls, otters, mink, foxes and seals, to name just some. But of course, the trout's greatest enemy is man.

The evening was still lengthening as swallows soared and children played with hurling sticks at crossroads. When we reached home, the Angelus was beating out from the car radio and the doctor went wordlessly inside. We had not spoken on the journey, which, even accounting for the radio, was unusual. He was tired, I reasoned, as I tried to reroute the cause of his ominous mood away from the dangerous territory of earlier events.

The telephone rang. Only the hospital in Clonmel called at this time, or a patient who owned a telephone. Or Father McVee. I listened at the door to the hall.

'No doubt, no doubt. And I hope you kill the one I lost the other evening, but count me out tonight, Father. There's something here I really must attend to.'

My stomach sank and I began to shiver. I had hoped that after supper he would go fishing, for even though that meant he would be with Father McVee, when he was with the priest the danger to me seemed somehow neutralized. Deciding to play to the earlier perception that I was coming down with flu, I went to my bedroom. Thirty minutes later, as I lay beneath the covers, I heard the doctor's step on the stairs. I began to shiver in earnest, as if the diverting illness could be summoned at will. My teeth were chattering.

'So this is where you are, Alex. Let's have a look at you.'

He drew down the bedclothes, opened my pyjamas and placed the stethoscope on my chest. He made me sit up, then listened through my back, took my pulse, examined my tongue, my throat, my ears; even my hands. Sitting on the bed, he looked curiously at me.

'Mmmm.'

I felt powerless beneath his unbending scrutiny.

'You don't have the flu.'

My skin retracted and I tried to cough.

'We need to have a little chat.'

Lost in an all-engulfing tide of misery, I tried to retch, as if a good show of vomit might make him back off.

'It's all right, Alex, I think I understand.'

That my father could never begin to understand only deepened the crisis. I began to weep.

'It was that boy, wasn't it?'

I nodded. I had no idea what he was going to say next.

'I believe his name is Terence. Well, I've been thinking a lot about this afternoon, about Terence trying to run away—but of course I can only guess at why. Did he talk to you? Did Terence tell you things? Did he say why he was running away?'

I found myself pitched into a terrifying void.

'What did Terence tell you, Alex?'

'Nothing.'

'I'm a doctor as well as your father. Nothing you will say can surprise me or make me cross. Do you understand that? Nothing.'

How wrong he was, how wrong.

In a voice as tender as the one he had used on the morning he had gone to Dublin, he said: 'You're an innocent little lad. You've spent all your life here with me. The world is a nasty place. Bad things happen. Bad people do dirty things.'

I clutched myself and cried inconsolably, for my secret was unfolding and soon I would be less than filth before him.

'Did Terence tell you about dirty things going on? Did he, Alex?'

Tears splashed on my cheeks.

'No.'

But the doctor caught my chin and turned my face to his.

'Is that the truth, Alex? I don't think so. Tell me what Terence told you. Something bad's going on there, isn't it? With his uncle? I want the truth.'

As his questions fell on me, as the vacuum through

which I tumbled resounded with ugly noises, I suddenly looked into the doctor's penetrating glare and saw my escape.

'I have come across this before. A defenceless boy in the care of an old, childless man whose wife is sick, or in some cases, deceased. What happens is a vile sin. I've read about it. In this case, I've seen the way he looks at the boy, the way he touches him... This is to help Terence, Alex. You must help him. You must tell me.'

As I began to grasp that the most appalling solution to my dilemma had been presented, appalling but complete, I nodded dumbly.

'I need to be clear about this, because there will be consequences.' The doctor looked at me and smiled reassuringly. 'But you don't have to worry—it's not your fault, any more than it's Terence's. This will have to be stopped, you understand? Now, tell me: did Terence try to run away because his uncle is doing dirty things to him?'

All I could think of was what the doctor would do if he found out from me about Father McVee. I sank my head and mumbled, 'Yes.'

'Lord have mercy on us!' He stood up and I thought it was over, but he was fishing in the pocket of his jacket for his rosary beads. 'We're going to say a decade of the rosary, Alex. We're going to offer it up for Terence.'

With that, he knelt down beside the bed and led off with the 'Our Father'.

The shared prayers worked their calmness. Gradually I realized that the dire threat to me had been transformed and that my problem was at an end. It was just another case in the doctor's busy day. The next day would be no different, nor the weeks and years ahead. I had grasped the outline of how life proceeds, and how some survive the dangers that emerge along the way, and how some do not.

28

Leaves scurried like tadpoles along the laneways as autumn wind hissed in the ditches. At four on a late October afternoon I was walking home from school, schoolbag on my back. I had grown that summer, filled out, shot up by more than an inch and passed the point of being a very young boy. Sometimes I thought of Flannery's and of what had taken place there, but never for long. The doctor had not mentioned the matter again and I occasionally relished the thought of how easily in the end I had slipped the knot that had once bound me. Terence's anguished face had faded too, like the fallen leaves.

As rain spat, a car came up behind. I stuck out my arm for a lift. Father McVee was hunched forward in concentration, hands high on the steering wheel. If he saw me, he made no sign of it. The wind strengthened.

His visits had become less frequent; the fishing season was nearly over. When I reached home, wind in my ears, his car was outside the hall door. I made my way around the gable and in by the back door. Some evenings, when the doctor was out and Mrs Tyrrell had gone home, I thumbed through the doctor's diary to see if he had attended Mrs Flannery. I was not sure why I needed to confirm this fact: it was as if the absence of the name brought further confirmation that nothing had changed. I put down my schoolbag and listened. The house was silent: Thursday was Mrs Tyrrell's half-day. From the long, hall mirror that faced the back door my reflection looked at me: tall, all at once, bare knees that stood out awkwardly, fair hair in need of a cut. Then the doctor's voice came from the sitting room.

'You must have got an awful shock.'

Moving closer to the hall, I heard the sound of a bottle being unstoppered. The priest said, 'It was a dreadful sight entirely. God be merciful to him.'

'Where did he do it?'

'In an outhouse. From the beam where he used to hang his waders.'

'God have mercy on his soul. And on his poor wife.'

'She found him. She's staying with neighbours. I doubt she'll ever go back there.'

I slid down to the floor, knees to my chin. From where I sat, I could see out through the window in the back door to where the autumn sun was slanting across the upper boughs of an old apple tree, illuminating the fruit that still clung there. I heard the men going out by the hall. Ghost-like, I made my way to the window in the hallway.

'There's a little pool up from Mahon Bridge that needs our attention next season,' Father McVee said.

The doctor chuckled and I could hear the pipe stem rattle on his teeth. 'Is there no fish in the county safe from you, Father?'

The priest's reply was lost in the sound of his feet on the gravel. He had reached his car when the doctor said, 'This incident does remove any doubt, doesn't it?'

The priest turned.

'I have to say, when I first made the complaint back in the summer, I had some doubts,' the doctor said. 'You know, he always seemed a decent sort.'

From my position, I could see both the doctor and the priest. At that moment, for just the merest instant, a look of naked guilt seized Father McVee and he stood by his car, transfixed. I looked at my father. He too, for that short moment, appeared to have seen the same thing, for he abruptly turned his gaze to the ground and coughed, removing the pipe from his mouth.

'But this confirms it beyond question, as far as I'm concerned,' he mumbled.

'Ach, you did the right thing, doctor, rest assured,' responded the priest, as if freed from his immobility. 'The boy's far better off in Clonmel, out of harm's way.'

The doctor shook his head grimly.

'It's a very sad case indeed,' he said.

Adult female mayflies, in their dun stage, leave the surface of the water in which they have spent their lives, and fly to dry land. There, after several days, they moult again. Males swarm thickly above the trees and bushes where the females are hiding. When the females fly up, a spectacular mating dance occurs. The males immediately die. The females follow the current upstream and lay their eggs on a suitable stretch of water. They too die and then drift downstream on the surface of the water.

The eggs that escape being consumed by trout fall to the riverbed, where they become nymphs—and the cycle begins again.

28

'Terence went into the industrial school in Clonmel,' Brother Malachy says. 'Charlie McVee taught him Christian doctrine and prepared him for his Intermediate Certificate.'

'Did McVee... did he continue...?'

'I don't think so, or at least he didn't admit it to me. Although he was defiant to the end about his relationship with children, he felt genuine remorse about Flannery. He said that over and over.'

'What happened to Terence?'

'His aunt left the farm to the parish and Terence went on to become a priest.'

'A *priest!*'

'He had to go to America to be ordained, of course. It would have been difficult here—with his background.'

'You say America. Do you know what diocese he was in?'

'He ended up in Detroit, I think... Yes, Detroit, Michigan, the place all the cars are made. I remember hearing it from a priest who was here on retreat. The diocese was Saint Patrick's, he said, and Terence went by the name of Father Thomas Deasy.'

As autumn gave way to winter, I sometimes thought about Terence, but when I did my mind veered almost immediately to Mr Flannery. He was wide and guileless, open, tender and full of bewildered love and compassion. Death was a strange, neutral thing, with no bearing on me or my world. Sometimes I dreamed that dead Mr Flannery's hairy arm was resting on Terence's neck and Terence was snuggling into his uncle's chest. They seemed to love each other, even though one of them was dead. Sometimes, dead Mr Flannery was shutting the dog back in the shed. More often, though, he was hanging, his heels kicking, just like his thigh-waders had done when I had imagined them to be a man.

The sun is slipping behind the peak that looms over Wilkins Abbey. Rooks thrash in high trees as wind scours the mountain.

'Did he have any visitors here?' I ask as Brother Malachy locks the door to his canteen and we walk back up the path towards the arch.

'Other than the guards?' Brother Malachy sighs. 'There was one old man, a priest from Waterford, came up to see him a couple of times. He was in a wheelchair because he had a bad heart condition. Other than him, no one.'

'How did he die?'

'Peacefully. We anointed him, of course, and it looked like he might rally, as he had before, but no. He just went off in a matter of hours.' Brother Malachy chuckles. 'And you know something, Alex? I grieved.'

My face must show my surprise.

'Yes, I grieved when Charlie McVee died. The day we buried him, I burnt everything. His clothes, bedding, shoes, books—everything. I spent the whole next day cleaning out his cell. I could not believe that he was gone. He was the scum of God's earth, but it is still God's earth.'

As I drive away, he stands in the arch, hands tucked into the sleeves of his robe. He came up here to this lonely place as a young man and fell in love. When he dies, his possessions will be sent to his next of kin in a shoebox.

Dusk is gathering, as I slip towards the coast, as if sinking to the seabed. I once made this journey before. Foam rides over the sea wall in Dungarvan and the thick black cliff of the Waterford coast is like a line drawn on a canvas.

The trout, like all fish, is cold-blooded, which means that his metabolism and, consequently, his level of activity depend directly on the temperature of the water. When the temperature is average, he is at his best, hunting eagerly and growing rapidly to manhood. But if his surroundings become too hot or too cold, if the environment turns against him, he simply dies.

PART THREE

Waterford, Ireland

1970

1

I took the stairs up to the landing, two at a time. The January sky, seen through the big window, hung low over the town. Saturday classes had ended and we had been given permission to go for lunch with my father on my eighteenth birthday.

Seán Phelan was at the boot rack, working a duster over his toecaps.

'We'd better not be late,' I said, 'he's always on time.'

'God forbid we'd keep the doctor waiting,' Seán said. A spear of sunlight cut into his blond curls. He looked no more than sixteen. He picked up his biretta and we clattered down to the front door.

'What did Nugent say?' Seán asked.

'That we have to be back at five for Adoration,' I said.

'Fair play to you,' Seán said.

We had been in the same class in Carrick, and done the Leaving Cert together the previous summer, but had not been friends. My father had discouraged me from mixing with the children of his patients. He considered dairy farmers like the Phelans, who could as equally as him afford the fees to send their son to a Catholic seminary, unsuitable company. And yet, on my first day in Waterford, when the doctor had left me off at the college, and shook my hand, and stood, his chin thrust out, watching me climb the steps with my suitcase as if I were ascending to heaven, when the doors opened and I saw Seán Phelan my heart had lifted.

A red Humber, our new car, was parked below the front door. The bodywork was buffed and polished, even though the journey south from Carrick in that morning's rain must have been mucky. The doctor had driven down early, I realized, and had had the car washed. As he stepped from it, wearing the green and yellow tweed suit I knew he kept for good wear, his eyes narrowed when he saw who I was with.

'Congratulations,' he said stiffly and shook my hand. 'Happy birthday.'

'Dad, this is Seán Phelan—we're in the same class. Is it all right if he joins us?'

'Ah,' he said, taking in Seán's black cassock and biretta. 'How do you do... Brother Phelan?'

'Delighted to meet you again, Doctor Smyth,' said Seán and they shook hands. 'Thanks for inviting me.'

My father's expression, which I could read like a page, contained multiple reservations, beginning with who Seán was and ending with the fact that the doctor had not invited him; sandwiched in between was my father's indissoluble respect for the clergy.

'I've only booked for two,' he said and looked at me sharply.

'Sure, there's only two of us,' said Seán cheerfully and clambered into the back of the car.

As we drove out by the gardens with their neatly

aligned paths, and began the short drive to the Tower Hotel, I played to my father's need to be vicariously associated with my new life, describing for him the progress of our pastoral formation, and the lectures we had been given by senior clerical figures, some of them from Rome. At the hotel, a porter held open the door and the doctor stood back to allow us in before him. In the lounge, he ordered cordials for us and a whiskey for himself as he amended the luncheon booking.

'They're the two great vocations, you know,' he said to Seán as the first sip of whiskey flushed his cheeks. 'Medicine and the Church—but of the two, yours is by far the greater.'

I sat back as he laid out for Seán his theories on poverty and injustice, arguments I had heard from my childhood. The doctor had already remade Seán as a priest, which instantly forgave my friend all the other shortcomings that had up to so recently defined him.

A tall, wheezing head-waiter, with smooth black hair and dressed in a dinner jacket, approached.

'Whenever you're ready, doctor.'

We followed him into the busy dining room.

'Do you fish at all, Brother?' I heard my father asking.

'With all the milking, I never had the time, doctor,' Seán replied.

'Ah, the beauty of it,' my father said and shook his head with pleasure. 'Some of the best moments of my life have been spent on that river. Father McVee is a passionate fisherman—did you know that?'

'I've heard he is, all right,' Seán said.

At a window table overlooking Reginald's Tower, the head-waiter handed me a menu and said, 'Soup of the day is mushroom, Father.'

I stole a glance across the table. Seán was biting his lip to prevent himself from laughing, but the doctor's face shone with pride.

2

I thought a lot about the doctor during those first months in Waterford, trying to see if by dissecting him more I could understand him better. An only child, like me, my father had been brought up in a household where social standing in the local community was of the utmost importance. I gathered from the way he spoke in admiring terms of her eccentricities that my grandmother had been a formidable snob. Her family had owned a drapery shop in Waterford; her marriage to my grandfather, a farmer with a small holding, albeit a fine, handsome man, had been deemed highly unsuitable. Why then had she married him? It seemed likely, although this was a question I could never ask, that she had been forced to do so. If this was the case, the only explanation for it in the Ireland of the 1920s was that my grandmother had been pregnant.

The doctor often spoke of his own father in terms of disparagement, saying that all the brains came from his mother's side. She had insisted the servants and farm-hands address her as 'madam' and her son, my father, as 'Master Patrick'. She had never taken a meal in the kitchen, or allowed her son to do so. Her husband, who had been brought up eating in the kitchen, seemed to have been treated by his wife like a common labourer.

My father was educated at home by a private tutor until the age of twelve when he was sent off to Rockwell College in County Tipperary. His mother told him that the only two professions worthy of him were the church or medicine. His prejudices had been engraved from a very early age. His mother died when he was in medical school, and a few years later, his father was diagnosed with dementia. The young doctor, as he was by then, booked his ailing father into the county home, sold the house and farm where he had grown up and acquired a fine residence on five acres, overlooking the River Suir on the outskirts of Carrick.

3

Seán Phelan and I did everything together, except sleep. We met each morning at Lauds, knelt side by side at Mass, were served at the same table for breakfast and sat at two adjoining desks in the classroom. We played hurling, ran, adored the Blessed Sacrament, went to Benediction, said the rosary and had evening cocoa together. The other seminarians called us the Carrick lads. In our private time, we discussed prayer, meditation and contemplation, the Scriptures, Jeremiah's call and response, and the lives and idiosyncrasies of the other priests, deacons and seminarians with whom we lived. I came to rely on the comfort of prayer, the penetrating sense of security found in an empty church and the great mystery of faith to which I had been admitted.

In that winter's first fall of snow, as we turned left at the estate wall and Seán quickened the pace, we suddenly came within sight of Woodstown Beach. Seán, who was stringy of build and ran with his head swinging doggedly from side to side, had won inter-county athletics medals in school and had now persuaded Father Nugent, the Vice-Rector and Dean of Students, to let us do road training. We stopped on a crescent of sand below the dunes, hands on our knees, gulping air, as gulls swooped over the low-tide cockleshells.

'I'd nearly go for a swim,' he said.

'Swim on your own,' I said, brushing snow from my hair.

The rotting poles of net fishermen marched to the distant tide as I huddled into the side of a sand dune and Seán scooped snow from the pampas grass and tried to drink it. In a brief clearance, the gable end of a building appeared fifty yards away. Its painted sign said, 'The Saratoga'.

'We need a drink,' Seán said.

'I brought no money.'

'I have money. Come on.'

Only when his professional services were required did the doctor ever enter a public house. Occasionally, if his visit there had been arduous, he would accept a whiskey from the owner. At such times, I would be brought in from the car and given lemonade.

A strong gust flung the Saratoga's door inwards. Linoleum covered the floor and the deserted wooden counter gleamed like bone from the glow of a night-light placed on the mantelpiece beneath a picture of the Sacred Heart and a large photograph of Mrs Jacqueline Onassis.

'Let's go,' I said, seeing the place was empty, but Seán rapped on the counter.

A door slammed and a woman wearing a heavy brown overcoat appeared behind the bar.

'Jesus,' she said, 'how did you two get here?'

'We got caught in the snow, ma'am,' Seán said, and then, 'two large bottles please. And ten Carrolls.'

142

She looked at us closely and pointed at me. 'He's okay,' she said to Seán, 'but how old are you?'

'I'm older than him,' Seán said. 'I swear.'

'Christ,' she said and shivered, 'would you ever pull the other one?'

Seán had a cigarette in his mouth as he poured his drink sideways into his glass.

'Sláinte,' he nodded and drank thirstily.

The drink was so bitter I gagged; I had never tasted alcohol before. The woman was plugging in a one-bar fire beside the chimney breast.

'You two brats are going to get pneumonia,' she said, pulling her coat tightly around her as she shuffled off.

Seán raised his glass towards the mantelpiece. 'To Jackie,' he said, 'the world's most beautiful woman.'

Jackie O seemed to be looking down at us.

'I saw her three years ago, walking down the beach outside,' Seán said, smacking his lips. He offered me a cigarette. 'She walked this near to me and when I said hello, she turned and smiled at me.'

'Get away! Jackie O?'

'I'm telling you. She wasn't Jackie O then, though, she was still Jackie Kennedy. My father drove us down on a Sunday morning after Mass, and there she was, boy. Of course, there were Secret Service fellas behind her, and lots of other people like us, gawking, but she'd come down to the beach from the big house for a walk, on her own, and there she was, right here, boy, on Woodstown beach, JFK's widow, as near to me as the counter.'

I looked up at the photograph. 'She's so beautiful.'

'I couldn't breathe, boy. And the way she walked, striding out, like a beautiful cat. For a year after, every night I went to sleep with Jackie in my arms.'

A door slammed again and the woman reappeared carrying a tray with two steaming glasses.

'Now, lads,' she said, 'get these into ye. I can't have ye going home to your mothers frozen.'

After the bitter stout, the whiskey slipped down sweet and easy. I leaned back, inhaling smoke, as my blood began to quicken and the image of the beautiful raven-haired woman in the photograph swamped my senses. Seán's glass was cupped between his hands as he stared at the red bar of the fire.

'It's the one thing they keep going on about, isn't it?' he said. 'That God's grace can accomplish all things. That with Jesus' cross we can overcome sex and live our lives without torture.'

Condensation had begun to rise from our wet running clothes.

'Do you believe them?' I asked.

'Celibacy is a declaration that the greatest joys are to be found not in earthly goods but in union with God in this life and in the next.'

'I didn't ask you to quote from one of Nugent's classes,' I said. 'I asked, do you believe them?'

Seán had finished his whiskey and had taken up the stout bottle again.

'My relationship with Jesus is the most important thing in my life,' he said, 'and so, whatever it takes, I'll hang in there.'

As the first wave ever of being tipsy washed through me, I felt the sudden need to talk.

'Sometimes…'

Seán looked at me. 'What?'

'This sounds crazy.'

'Go on.'

'I sometimes… I sometimes think there's someone else inside me.'

'Inside you?'

'Yes, someone I've never met.'

Seán blew smoke from the side of his mouth. 'Are you serious?'

'Yes. He's someone bad, someone who's done a really bad thing.'

Seán was looking at me sceptically. 'Such as?'

I struggled to see. 'I don't know.'

'Yes, you do! Go on!'

With my eyes closed, I said, 'Killed a person.'

Seán burst out laughing.

'It's not funny,' I said as the desperate need to confide overwhelmed me. 'I have these bad dreams. I'm often scared to sleep, because they're really terrifying. Dogs are tearing me apart. It's because I'm guilty…'

'Look, I have bad dreams too. Dreams that my parents are dead. Dreams that my legs are being cut off in a combine harvester.'

'I have dreams about Father McVee,' I heard myself say.

Seán frowned. 'About our Father McVee? Our parish priest?'

'Yes.'

'What kind of dreams?'

As if alcohol had sparked a light in my brain, I said, 'Can I tell you something you must never tell anyone?'

'What?'

'You must promise.'

'I promise—now, what?'

'As if you were hearing my confession,' I said.

'Jesus, Alex, this would want to be good. What?'

I took a deep breath. 'I think Father McVee is a dirty old man.'

Seán Phelan rocked back in his chair and put down his glass. '*What?*'

'I think he does dirty things with children. With boys.'

'My God, Alex, that's a very serious accusation.'

'I know.'

'Are you saying he did things to you?' Seán asked.

'No, I'm not. He didn't.'

'So, why are you saying it?'

'I just know.'

'You'd want to be careful what you say. Did somebody else give you this information?' Seán had gathered himself. 'Has someone, another lad, made this accusation about our parish priest?'

As suddenly as it had gone on, the light in my mind went out and I was floundering. I turned my face away because I was going to cry and couldn't stop myself. I wiped my nose on the sleeve of my running shirt and tried to stop.

'Alex?'

'Forget it, I'm sorry. It was just the drink talking.'

'Listen to me now,' Seán said sternly. 'Father McVee gave me my First Holy Communion. He anointed both my grandparents. When my sister got scarlet fever and was a month in the hospital in Clonmel and we all

146

thought she was dying, Father McVee went in to see her every day and sat beside her, even though he might have picked up her infection. And, as far as I know, he wrote you a glowing reference for the seminary—am I right?'

'Yes.' All of a sudden the stout and whiskey had given me the beginnings of a bad headache. 'Forget everything I said.'

'Alex, look at me, please.'

Seán had knelt down and had placed his hands on my shoulders.

'Look at me!'

I felt that I had lost something important, but had no idea how to get it back.

'We all have these dreams,' Seán said urgently. 'Sex tries to do in our heads and makes us imagine the worst in everyone. Our imagination goes mad, just as yours did a minute ago. Sex makes us want to kill ourselves for the bad thoughts we have indulged in. That's why you think there's a killer inside you! It's you, Alex, trying to kill yourself for your impure thoughts!'

My head spun.

'Everything we dream about is ourselves in a different disguise—do you not remember Nugent's lectures?' Seán asked.

I nodded.

'So when you dream that Father McVee is a dirty old man, it's *you* who is the dirty old man, Alex—can you see that? It's you who are doing dirty things, in your dreams, with other boys, not Father McVee. That's the devil's way of trying to snare you. He sneaks into your bed, into your mind when you're asleep and plays every trick he

147

knows to make you commit a sin. It's very important that you understand that, Alex, and that you never ever again say what you've just said to me.'

He was gripping my shoulders tightly.

'Every one of us in the seminary goes through something like you're going through. It's natural—we're young healthy men. But here's what I'm going to tell you. You and I came into this together and we're going to come out of it together. Okay? We're a team. Any time you want to tell me about your dreams, that's okay too. Have we a deal?'

I nodded, mutely.

'Come here to me.'

He hugged me close to him, his ginger stubble on my neck, as Christ and Jackie O looked on and I could see light glinting in the far window as a clearance crept up the estuary.

4

I could not shake off a feeling of despondency that overtook me every time my father came to mind. It was as if he would always represent something dark that could be understood only by a part of me that had been buried beyond my reach. My dreams, which I never mentioned again to Seán, continued. The doctor and Father McVee would appear, riding a white horse together. Or they were on a train pulling out of Kilkenny station, just as I arrived. Or I was gliding down a river, not of water but of leaves. The day was warm and I had peeled off my clothes. Suddenly, the wooden deck of the boat ruptured and a crab apple tree pushed into view, growing powerfully even as I watched it. Sexual longing swept through me. But the boat had begun to sink and I could not swim.

It would take another forty-five years for me to understand what these dreams were about.

5

The bus pulled up in sunshine at the front steps of the seminary and we climbed on, each with a bag for his sports clothes. Women from the kitchen carried out picnic hampers and loaded them. We headed down the Mall, across the Manor and out the Tramore road. I sat beside a man from Ferrybank, Anthony Butler, whose uncle was a bishop somewhere in Africa. Anthony said little and was slight of build. I spent the twenty-minute journey looking at the photographs of an African village that his uncle had sent him and of which Anthony was shyly proud.

I had done well in my exams but I was not looking forward to the summer holidays. In August the college was closing and everyone was going home for three weeks. The prospect of three weeks with my father in Carrick dismayed me, which in turn made me feel ashamed.

We must have presented a strange spectacle that day as we disembarked at the end of the promenade: over thirty young men in Roman cassocks and birettas, heading at speed like a gaggle of black geese for the Rabbit Burrows. In sand dunes, a mile from the town, we changed into football jerseys and shorts. Senior seminarians arranged us into four teams and laid stones out on the strand to mark the pitches. The Whit Monday seven-a-side Gaelic football game had been going for years.

We ran at each other, roaring for the ball and howling when it went into the sea. Occasionally, local people who had walked this far down the strand paused to watch us. We played fifteen minutes a side, then, boiling and sweaty, ripped off our jerseys, runners and socks and charged like mad men into the surf. Since I could not swim, I went out only to my waist and splashed around, while others, like Seán, made a point of heading for the horizon. I watched as his body sliced through the waves like a white fish.

Anthony Butler couldn't swim either so he and I walked back in towards the shore and stood in the shallow water. I remember the glad sun on my chest and the pounding of the tide. I closed my eyes and when I opened them again, Anthony was gone. I turned and saw him hurrying back into the sand dunes. And then I saw three girls, standing twenty yards away, watching what was going on.

The sea breeze had blown their hair back from their faces and had wrapped their summer skirts tight to their legs. I felt my skin prickling. They were laughing quietly as they resumed their walk and in a moment or so would pass me. I stared. The girl nearest to me had long black hair. She was taller than the others and her figure was deliciously formed. She was so beautiful she could have been Jackie O. As she passed within two yards, she looked straight at me and smiled. Her eyes were sea-deep green. Then, as if someone so beautiful could not bear to exist for more than a second, she was gone, back up the strand, striding out like a beautiful cat, and I was left standing in the tide.

The seminary was renowned for its food, the produce of its out-farms. Plates of sliced pork, cured ham and pressed tongue were laid out on white tablecloths in the lee of the sand dunes. We poured home-made lemonade from glass bottles. Some of the lads had gathered flotsam for a fire and we boiled up the water we had brought.

I had known for thirty minutes that I had made the wrong choice in life. Something fundamental had changed. I saw the other lads, up to this morning my close companions, as strangers. Later, as we changed back into our cassocks, shoes and birettas, collected up the picnic things and made our way up the strand to the bus, I was overwhelmed by what had happened. A primal message had been conveyed to me and I had become aware of my extraordinary new potential.

'You're very quiet,' Seán said as we lined up to get the bus. 'Are you all right?'

'I don't know,' I said. 'I may have caught something.'

In June we made hay on the college farm near Cheekpoint, and stayed in a draughty old house that looked back up the river towards Waterford. The brothers who ran the farm reared pigs and I helped them with the birthing sows around whose udders the blind piglets poked and sucked.

I did not know what to do or how to disentangle myself. My greatest dread was my father, for I knew that he would never understand or accept my changed position. I went back to the seminary to see Father Nugent, a caring man in his early fifties, who had once played hurling with some distinction. He offered me a cigarette and we both composed ourselves in a cloud of smoke. I wanted to discuss my dilemma only in general terms, for I feared that if I told the truth, my father would find out.

'There is no shame to feel you may be called to the religious life and then discover you were mistaken,' Father Nugent said. 'The real shame, Alex, is to be called and not to answer.'

'Sometimes... it's just that I sometimes wonder if I'm in the right place.'

'One of our great strengths lies in numbers,' Father Nugent said. 'Over four hundred thousand of us worldwide, every one of whom has at some point asked himself the questions you're now asking. Look around you and every priest you see, including yours truly, has had enormous doubts about whether or not he's in the right place. Think of the priests you have known growing up as a child in Carrick: it's the same for them. Your own parish priest, Father Charles McVee, wrote your letter of reference when you applied to come here. Even Father McVee will have had doubts about his vocation, but has overcome them to live a healthy life of prayerful watchfulness in union with God.'

Father Nugent got a fit of coughing that bent him in two.

'I'll have to give these up,' he gasped, 'and with the help of God I will.' He walked me to the door of his study. 'Would it help you to have a chat with Father

McVee about this whole matter? He's a very good man and a personal friend of mine. I could give him a ring and I'm sure he'd be only too happy to oblige.'

'Thank you, Father, but I'd prefer we kept this between the two of us.'

'Of course, of course. Remember Saint Luke, Alex,' Father Nugent said, taking my hands in his. '"Any who do not carry their cross and come after me cannot be my disciple".'

I returned to Cheekpoint that evening. I stepped down from the bus and walked to the end of the long avenue to find Seán Phelan, standing at the door, waiting.

'Did you hear the news?' he asked.

'What news?'

'About Nugent?'

'I met Nugent earlier. We had a fag together.'

'He's in intensive care in Ardkeen Hospital,' Seán said. 'Heart attack. Not expected to live.'

6

On a hot July day, as Seán and I walked out the Dunmore Road, the smell of the river at low tide floated over the town. From an abattoir on the far bank, we could hear the squeals of pigs as they met their end. Father Nugent had been transferred to a nursing home for recuperation. We had prayed at his bedside in hospital when he had been anointed; but now he was able to walk a few steps and sit outside in a wheelchair.

'You're very quiet these days,' Seán said as we turned into Maypark Lane.

'I'm just thinking.'

'Remember our deal,' he said.

I felt the burden of my deceit and wondered if the change in me was obvious.

'Can I tell you something?' Seán asked. 'Something I've never told anyone?'

We had come to a small factory and stopped by the low wall that divided it from the road.

'Like everyone, I... you know, have bad thoughts. Dirty thoughts. My body goes mad.'

'Seán, you don't have to tell me...'

'I want to tell you! You see, I know that it's Satan in the bed beside me, but even though I pray, he won't go away. I can't sleep. D'you know what I do?'

I shook my head.

'I take out the noggin I have hidden in my shirt drawer, and I drink it.'

'You drink what?'

'Vodka,' he said and his expression was that of a man imparting great news. 'Neat vodka. It works wonders. Twenty minutes, I'm asleep.'

I stared at him. 'You mean, you get drunk and pass out?'

'Look, getting drunk is a far less serious sin than letting Satan take over your body. I'm a soldier in an army marching for the greatest cause the world has ever known. I fight with every means at my disposal. Sometimes it's not pretty—but in the end I'm still a soldier, still in the army. Christ's army.'

Trees overhung the driveway to the nursing home. On a lawn, where white wooden seats were laid out, patients sat with their visitors. Father Nugent, wearing a dressing gown, slippers and a white peaked cap, was parked to one side in the shade.

'Hello, boys.'

Seán had stopped at a shop on the way and bought cigarettes.

'Oh, Lord, if they see me smoking they'll kill me,' the priest said. 'Push me round the side of the house, there's a good lad.'

I stood back as Seán steered the wheelchair under a rose trellis. As I prepared to follow, a slender figure in a nurse's uniform appeared from the nursing home. Her black hair was tied up beneath a white cap. I felt myself begin to tremble. Her hand went to her mouth and she stared.

'Hello,' I said.

'You... oh, I'm so sorry,' she said.

'For what?'

She was looking at my cassock. 'You're... you're a priest.'

'I'm not, I'm really not. My name is Alex.'

'I'm very sorry,' she said, but we knew that up to that moment our encounter on the strand had been alive for both of us. 'I didn't know.'

'I need to tell you something.'

She frowned. 'What?'

'I have to see you.'

'I beg your pardon?'

'You need to understand something.'

She shook her head. 'Alex, I think you'd better go round the back for a smoke with your friend and Father Nugent.'

'On the strand that day, something happened, am I right? To both of us.'

'God, this is so embarrassing,' she said in a lowered voice. 'Would you please go away?'

'Please tell me your name.'

'Look, it was a mistake—can we leave it at that?'

'Please.'

'No!'

'Since that day I've thought about you every minute,' I said.

'Oh, God!'

'I'm completely serious. I've thought of nothing else. Nothing is more important to me.'

'It was... stupid. All right? Now I'm very busy, as you can see.'

'Please listen. I'm leaving the seminary.'

She blew out her cheeks.

I said: 'No one else knows that. There'll be murder, but I don't care.'

'I don't believe this,' she said.

'My only mistake was thinking I wanted to be a priest.'

She put one hand on her hip. 'Do you go on like this with every woman you meet?'

'Please!'

I could see people looking at us.

'This is crazy!' she whispered and tried to laugh. 'Go away!'

'Please.' I could hear the wheel rims of Father Nugent's wheelchair on the gravel. 'Give me one chance.'

Father Nugent was having another fit of coughing.

'Alex! Where were you?' I heard Seán calling.

'Just tell me your name!'

'God,' she said. 'My name is Kay.'

8

The Woodstown bus left clouds of airborne exhaust at every bend. It was Friday, the last day of July. I had written to my father telling him that I was not coming home, for reasons I would explain later.

Seán Phelan's parents had rented a house in Tramore for the month of August. Seán was now the person I dreaded telling, almost more than the doctor.

'Let's go for a walk first,' I said when the bus dropped us off at the Saratoga.

'I thought we were coming out here to celebrate the end of term,' Seán said.

'Yes, but first let's walk.'

Shells crunched under our black shoes as Seán ducked his head into his chest and lit a cigarette.

'It's been a great year,' he said, striding out, 'and they say the first one is the hardest.'

In the dunes to our right, families sat with picnics and children rolled down steep banks of sand.

'I'm going to train at swimming every day of the holidays,' he said. 'There's a sponsored race from the Boat Cove to Brownstown Head and I'm going in for it. Over two miles, boy. We'll all have to grease up.' He inhaled smoke deeply. 'You could come down and go in one of the boats, Alex. How about it? Would you come? It's on the bank holiday weekend. You could take swimming lessons—now there's a good idea! How about it?'

'I can't come, Seán.'

'I know, I know, staying at home with the da. Why don't you bring him down for the day—a little outing. He can't work all the time. He could come in the boat too, if he wanted. He'd love it.'

'I'm not going home, Seán,' I said.

He frowned at me and pulled up. 'You're not?'

'No.'

'So where are you going?'

'I don't know,' I said and took a deep breath. 'You see, I've decided to leave the seminary.'

Seán Phelan's hand went to his mouth and he took two steps back. '*What?*'

'I'm telling the rector tomorrow.'

'You mean . . . you're transferring to Maynooth or someplace?'

'Seán, I'm finishing up, I'm leaving. It's over for me. You see, I'm sorry, but I've met someone I feel very strongly about. I'm out.'

9

She was the elder of two girls. Her father was deceased and her mother, a Waterford woman, was a teacher who had taken early retirement, Kay told me.

We walked down Maypark Lane to the river and sat on the side of a boat slip. When she had left school the year before, she had stopped going to Mass. This had upset her mother, who had never recovered from her husband's sudden death a decade before and still lived in a state of perpetual mourning. Kay had applied for trainee positions in Dublin hospitals.

The summer light was turning the river into amber. I could not take my eyes off her.

'She thinks I'm selfish to want a life outside her and the shadow of Daddy's death. She says the rosary every night, and anyone who's in the house has to get down on their knees and pray for the repose of Daddy's soul. I loved Daddy very much, but we live every day as if he only died yesterday.'

We made our way along a wooded path by the still water.

'Do you have a boyfriend?'

'Kind of.'

'Then I'm sorry, but I just had to meet you and have this conversation.'

We had come to a beech tree and sat down under its spreading branches. I took out cigarettes. I watched her put her head back against the tree as she let the smoke out in a long, slender tail. Her calm beauty made me already regret the moment when I would have to leave her.

'People won't like me,' I said. 'They'll think I'm letting them down. Waterford's a very small place. All I'll bring you is trouble.'

She looked at me steadily. 'I don't care what people think. I make up my own mind.'

In those heat-baked days of July, as the sweet smells of broom and roses defied anyone to remember winter, we took separate buses out to Tramore and walked down the strand to where we had first met. The tide was held up stiff by wind as tiny crabs scuttled for safety. In the lee of the dunes, I lit a fire using the stones and twigs left behind after our Whitsun picnic. Oystercatchers soared over the Backstrand.

'Life can't just end,' she said. 'Look at this!'

As night fell and we both knew the last buses were gone, we lay by the fire, looking at the stars. If we stretched high enough, the universe was within our grasp. Behind us, the sea lay flat and mesmerising. Seabirds bent in an arc over the night water, illuminated by the moon.

10

Seán Phelan began to suck in his breaths like someone having a seizure. The cigarette dropped from his fingers.

'Oh, no,' he said, 'oh, no you don't, Alex, no way. We have a deal, remember? We made it right over there in that pub. We're going to go through with this together, remember? So, no way, boy—understand? No fucking way!'

'Seán…'

He blinked rapidly as if something had just occurred to him.

'That time a couple of weeks ago… when you didn't show up for supper… when you said you'd got lost out walking…'

'Seán…'

'No fucking way!' he shouted. 'This is exactly the kind of thing that can happen if you're not prepared for it. Now we're going back into that bar and we're having a stiff drink and we're going to talk this thing through like you promised we would.'

'Sorry.'

'Can't you see?' he cried. 'This is the big test! Like what happened to Our Lord in the desert. Satan curled around him, wrapped himself around Our Saviour's legs and tried to bleed all the goodness out of him for one moment—one fucking moment!—of pleasurable sin! It's Satan's most devious trick. But Jesus knew this was his big test. He put Satan behind Him. So can you, Alex. All you have to do is get over this one test and the rest is easy!'

'This has nothing got to do with Satan,' I said.

But Seán had caught me by the arm and was trying to pull me in the direction of the pub. 'Come on, now, Alex. Enough of this bullshit! Come on!'

'No.' I shook myself free. 'I'm sorry, but I know what I'm going to do. I know what I want. Lots of people will think I've let them down, but fuck them. It's my life. Our life. Please accept that.'

'I don't believe this,' he said, looking away. 'Is this a joke? It is, isn't it? Tell me this is a joke.'

He turned away and I could see that he was trying to contain his tears.

'Seán… '

He gulped.

'We can still be friends… ' I began.

He sprang at me, his hands at my throat and I fell down on the hard sand. He began to punch me in the face.

'You fucking sniveller!' he shouted as I tasted blood. 'You traitor!'

I caught his wrist and we rolled down the slight incline. He kept pummelling my face. He caught my hair and jerked back my head to hit me again. I thumped him once, full on his jaw and he slumped over.

'Seán… are you all right?' I gasped. 'I'm sorry.'

He was up on his knees. 'All that stuff you told me,' he said with a choke in his voice, 'it was pure shite, wasn't it?'

'What stuff?'

'About there being a person inside you that you'd never met. *Do I sound crazy, Seán? I have these bad dreams all the time. I'm scared to go asleep. I think Father McVee is trying to kill me, Seán.*'

'Come on,' I said, 'you know that was just between us.'

'I know what shit smells like, Alex. It smells like you. You and your old man. You know what we used to say whenever he left our house? If Doctor Smyth sticks his nose up any higher, we'll have to get the door lintel raised! How many times did Doctor Smyth come in to see my little sister in Clonmel when we all thought she was dying? Not once. Not one fucking time. But Father McVee came in. Three or four times a week. And now you're trying to paint him as some kind of a monster? It's men like you who are the monsters, Alex, leading people on, saying bad things about good men, pretending to be friends when it suits you, making promises you can't keep. I would have trusted you with my life, you know that? *With my life.*'

If it wasn't for the image of Kay's luminous face, I would have walked into the estuary and drowned myself. Seán wiped his face with his handkerchief, blew his nose and straightened his hair.

'I'm amazed it took me so long to see it.' He rubbed his jaw. 'We never had this conversation. We were never out here today.'

'As you wish.'

'We never came out here last winter, or had a drink, or talked about our lives and made a pact,' he said as his face became set and he looked, in that moment, a much older person. 'I don't know what happened to you as a child, Alex, but whatever it was, you are the most fucked-up person I have ever met.'

I felt both desolate and elated.

'Seán… '

His back was to me. I held out my hand.

'We'll probably never speak again, but for old times' sake?'

'May God forgive you,' he said, 'because I don't think I can.'

He walked back towards the road. I could hear the cries of the children in the dunes, the screech of gulls and the thud of my soaring heart.

11

I often thought of the moment the doctor answered the telephone the following morning. It is the first of August. He's a man used to calls that bring bad news, but this is in a different category. When it is over, he sits down heavily, hollowed by what he has just been told.

His first reaction is to not believe it. He sees me as his ultimate project, someone he has not just begot but designed. I have gone seamlessly from school to seminary and passed my exams with distinction. Everything he has heard affirms my relentless progress towards achieving the greatest accolade he can imagine. Now this. A brief but decisive call. He is completely flattened.

But the doctor is not a man to lie down under misfortune for long. After my mother's death, he steeled himself, built up a flourishing medical practice and at the same time reared a child. Every day he must gird himself against the injustices of fate and social deprivation. Now this. After a few minutes, he gets up. He must brace himself again.

After Mass, everyone scrambled to get packed and gone. I made my way to the rector's office.

'Are you quite sure?' he asked, and when I said I was, he held out his hand. 'Goodbye, Alex.'

Dizzy, I walked down the corridor to the stairs that led up to the bedrooms and came face to face with Seán Phelan. I tried to say something but he averted his eyes and hurried past me. In my room, I left my cassock and biretta on the bed. I looked up and saw Anthony Butler standing at the door.

'Anthony, I'm… I don't know if you heard but… '

He looked at me despondently. 'It's not my fault, is it?'

'*Your* fault?'

'That day in Tramore… '

'What about it?'

'I saw what was going to happen, I saw it exactly. I wondered afterwards if I should have made you come with me,' he said. 'But I didn't. You stood your ground, I ran away.'

'It's okay, Anthony, really.'

He smiled. 'I bet I know which one of them it is. The tall one.'

'Yes.'

'I'm happy for you, Alex,' he said. 'She's lovely.'

I made it down to the garden level with my suitcase, took a deep breath and walked out. The first person I saw was the doctor. He was standing by the car, talking to the rector. They both turned when they saw me. The rector touched my father's elbow in a gesture of sympathy or conciliation, then, with a sad smile, went into the building. The doctor's hands had balled into fists and were level with his waistcoat.

'Hello, Alex.'

'Hello, Dad.'

'Are we going home, Alex?'

'I'd like that, Dad. Yes, please.'

He reached for my case. 'He's a most understanding man, your rector, you're blessed to have him here. A saint.'

I closed my eyes. 'He's told you.'

'We discussed you,' the doctor said busily, as he placed my case in the boot and slammed the lid.

'What did he say?'

'Oh, just that you'd had a little brainstorm, that's all—nothing he hasn't seen a hundred times before. Nothing that we can't work out between the lot of us. You can take a whole month off, he told me. What could be more generous?' The doctor was getting into the car. 'By the way, I meant to write and tell you, the trout at home these nights are lepping something unbelievable.'

'Dad.'

He frowned.

'Dad, I'm not coming back here. It's over. Sorry, but that's my decision.'

He got out of the car again and very carefully closed the door. 'What?'

'Dad, let me explain… '

'Just a moment, Alex, if you wouldn't mind. We've just dealt with all that, haven't we? Please don't make a fool of yourself twice in the same morning. Now get into the car. I have left sick people waiting in order to come down here. Get in, please!'

'I can't do that unless you accept my decision, Dad.'

His face darkened. 'Is this all the respect you have for

me, Alex? After all I've done for you? Brought you up on my own? Kept you by my side, given you everything you could want, loved you. I made huge sacrifices, you know. Is this the way you repay me?'

'If only you'd listen.'

'For what? To hear more lies?'

I shook my head. 'What lies?'

'Your letters telling me everything here was going so well. The promises you made to your friends.'

I realised then that Seán must have telephoned him. 'Everything I said was true at the time,' I said.

His mirthless laugh was the prelude to the eruptions I so feared. 'At least there are some decent lads here who understand how a father feels. A father who prayed he would get his reward in heaven and not a liar for a son.'

'Dad... '

'A liar is a bad trait,' he snarled. 'I told you that many years ago, but it seems my words fell on deaf ears.'

'If I ever told lies,' I said, 'it was only because I was too afraid of you to tell the truth.'

'Why this?' he asked and his face cracked in bewilderment. 'You have the whole world at your feet. Why?'

'Because I've met someone and fallen in love. Surely you can understand that, Dad?'

His lips came back from his teeth. 'What do you know of love?'

I knew it was hopeless then. 'Maybe in time you will understand,' I said.

'I'm giving you one last chance,' he said and took a

step towards me. 'Go back into that building and tell the rector that you made a mistake. Tell him you're sorry and that you're going home with me now, but that you're coming back here after the holidays. Tell him nothing has changed.'

I realized for the first time that I was a full head and shoulders taller than him. 'And if I don't?'

'Then,' he said and his whole body quivered, 'I don't have a son.'

I didn't believe him. 'Dad, I can't,' I said. 'The mistake would be to stay here.'

Breathing heavily, he went to the boot, opened it, took my suitcase and set it down on the gravel. He returned to the car, started up and shot down the avenue. I kept my back to the seminary as I picked up my case. Then I walked downhill as the smell of petrol still lingered, into the rest of my life.

Part Four

Ontario, Canada

Two years ago

1

The Air Canada flight from London touches down in Toronto Pearson shortly after three, local time. Instead of driving north for home, I head south-west on the 401. Because it's Friday evening, the traffic south is dense. The sun hangs in the sky like an apricot. Eventually, within sight of Lake Erie, the highway swings inland towards Windsor, where I get into a line for the border and sit there until the light ebbs.

You can't feel high blood pressure; you just suspect it. As I grew older, my panic attacks became worse, especially at night, to the point where Kay and I seldom slept in the same room. Now I crave the fresh air I left behind in Ireland. On the outskirts of Detroit, I pull in at the first motel and pay for a room. There's a tender quality to the sunset that is absent in midsummer, a blushing innocence. The street block is illuminated by only a single streetlight and long shadows rush out. A car cruises by, music from its radio seeping out in an invisible net.

It's dark outside as Kay goes to the kitchen, rummages in a deep drawer and finds cigarettes. She hasn't

175

smoked in thirty-three weeks. Through bared teeth she draws in the smoke with singular intent.

I have just called from a motel in Detroit.

'Detroit? Why are you in Detroit?'

'I'll try to explain.'

'You only called me once from Ireland.'

'I told you, I forgot to pack my charger.'

'Do they not have payphones in Ireland?'

'Not in the places I was. But listen, Larry is not this person. He's not Terence.'

'How do you know?'

'Because Terence became a priest. He worked in a number of U.S. dioceses, including Detroit. I looked him up on the Internet. He's in a diocese here called Saint Patrick's.'

Kay presses the bridge of her nose tightly. 'Do you have a photograph of him?' she asks. 'Of Terence?'

'No.'

'Jesus,' she says, 'I think you should come home. The strain of this is killing me.'

'I'll be home tomorrow.'

'I'm really feeling uncomfortable about Larry and whatever is going on, you know? Can you not come on home tonight?'

'I'm sorry, I just got here. I have to finish this. I'll call you in the morning.'

'Don't bother,' she said and hung up.

She's suddenly terrified, as if she has heard someone circling the house but cannot see him. She wonders if she should call Keith and ask him to come over—but what would he think of that request if she can't tell him what's going on? Or the Echenoz family? They're good neighbours, but the idea of landing in on them with such problems seems extreme. With a shock, Kay realizes she has no one to turn to.

Outside, night settles over Lake Muskoka.

2

In the early morning light yachts scurry in sunny clutches on Lake St Clair. It's just gone eight when I pull into the parking lot of Saint Patrick's church. Close by, linked to the church by a tree-lined path, stands the parochial office, a low building overlooking lawns. Fifty yards away, towards the boundary fence, in a grove set apart, are two houses with carports. Where the priests live.

I have repeated over and over to myself the words I'm going to say. *Terence, my name is Alex Smyth and I'm truly sorry for what happened.* What does he look like? Will he remember me? I get out of the car.

The quality of silence found in an empty church is always so reassuring. In the cool vestibule, floor-to-beam stained-glass windows scatter the sunlight in velvet cuttings.

'Good morning. Can I help you at all?'

A priest has emerged, smiling. Thick black eyebrows stand out, in contrast to his silver hair. He's a broad-shouldered man with a round face, a prominent nose. His age is difficult to pin down. I'm staring at him. His accent is Irish, or at least he speaks in the way of Irish people who have spent most of their lives in America.

'Father Deasy? Father Thomas Deasy?'

His smile disappears.

'Who wants him?'

'Alex Smyth is my name.'

It's him, I'm sure of it, even though I had expected Terence to be a man of bigger build and stature.

'Terence?'

The priest closes his eyes briefly in a gesture of impatience. 'My name is Father Denis Greely. Are you looking for Father Deasy?'

'I'm sorry,' I say, suddenly exhausted. 'Is he here?'

Father Greely shakes his head, as if in the short time we've met I have managed to exasperate him. 'Father Deasy hasn't lived or worked here for some time,' he says.

'His name is up on the parish website.'

'I don't care if it's up in Times Square, he isn't here,' the priest says.

'Do you know where he is?'

Father Greely sighs. 'What did you say your name is?'

'Alex. Alex Smyth. I'm Canadian. I've come here specially to find Father Deasy. We knew each other many years ago.'

'Mr Smyth, Father Deasy isn't well. But it's complicated. We're under instructions not to talk about him. All inquiries should be referred to the chancellery. Bishop Werner's orders. Now, if you'll please excuse me…'

'When you say he's not well…'

'He's got inoperable cancer. He's dying.'

I take a step back. 'I'm sorry, I didn't know.'

The priest shakes his head again. 'How could you have?'

'So he's in hospital?'

'You'll have to ask the bishop where he is. The number of the chancellery is right there, on the notice board. Now I have to go.'

'There are things I need to tell him,' I say as we step out into the warm sunshine.

'He got a raw deal,' the priest says.

I say, 'I know.'

3

The new Canadian day leaps out to the western horizon. In winter, fir and maple seem to be cut blackly from the cold sky, but in spring their branches and pliant young leaves ooze into the new air.

Kay is grim as she drives towards Roger's Quay. Five minutes ago she got a text from Tim saying 'gon watreskying', and now he's not answering. She blames Keith, who was meant to have shown up at the house earlier. Keith has no permission to bring Tim water-skiing. *I don't need this*, she thinks, *I really don't*.

If she could have another career, she thinks, it would be as an artist, living in Toronto, with maybe a couple of exhibitions a year. No trouble. An artistic life with like-minded friends. No baggage from someone else's life, which, it seems, she must always help to carry. Maybe it's too late for all that. Or maybe not. No one can go back, but, if she could, Kay thinks that she might take more time and do it differently.

She pulls up outside the wire-fenced boat compound and sees Keith on the jetty, in his usual blue overalls, loading a box of provisions onto a launch.

'Hi, Mrs Smyth!'

'Keith,' she says calmly, 'is Tim here?'

'Yes, ma'am.'

'How did he get here?'

'I drove him here, ma'am.'

'Damn it, he's not allowed here without one of us being told!' Kay says. She looks around. 'Where is he?'

'Waterskiin',' Keith replies.

'But… you're here. Who's he water-skiing with?'

'With Mr White. Doin' pretty good too.' Keith looks out to the lake. 'There they are now.'

Way out on the morning water, Kay can see two specks and a plume of foam.

'I want him to come back in,' she says and feels her legs weaken. 'Now.'

'I heard Mr White saying they were going back to the jetty at his place when they were through,' Keith says. 'You okay, ma'am?'

4

Twenty blocks go by before I can pick up the north-south highway. A little breeze is teasing out high branches and the hems of flags.

When I telephoned the chancellery, the call was diverted and then answered by a woman who spoke halting English. *Por favor, mantener la línea.* I was just about to hang up when a man's voice said 'Bishop Werner.'

In this upmarket, residential neighbourhood the houses are screened from view by tall fences or hedging. One tightly clipped and razor-topped line of verdure runs for almost fifty yards and ends in ten-foot high, gilt-tipped electric entrance gates that swing inwards when I press the bell. Dense shrubs mark one side of the driveway, and on the other, where an apron-like lawn sweeps down to the boundary of the property, wind-driven spray from a sprinkler system rinses upwards. The front door is carved from a yellowish wood with a theme of moons and stars set into the grain. A tiny, red activation beam shines like an eye from a high-mounted CCTV camera.

'I'm sorry about all the security—it's because of the insurance.'

The bishop is slightly built, stooped, sallow of

complexion, and wears spectacles that make him look short-sighted. He wears a priest's suit, a Roman collar and a small cross at his neck. He walks with the aid of a single crutch that props his right elbow. The hall is dominated by a life-size crucifix. To the left, two steps rise to an open door. A grand piano stands beneath an oil painting of the Virgin and Child.

'I've asked for tea to be brought to my study.'

Bishop Werner leads me through double doors and along a corridor to a book-lined room. Leather chairs with cushions are arranged around a low table.

'Do you take milk, Mr Smyth?'

'I don't, thank you, Bishop. And I'm Alex.'

'I'm Harald, or Hal, which I prefer to 'Bishop', although I'm afraid not many take me up on the offer.'

He pours the tea, sits back.

'So, Alex, Father Greely tells me that you were inquiring about Father Thomas Deasy.'

'Yes, Hal. But before we go any further, I wonder is it possible to see a recent photograph of Father Deasy? It's very important. I need to see it and then to make a phone call.'

The bishop looks mildly surprised, but gets back to his feet and makes his way slowly to an antique desk in the corner. From the bottom drawer, after some searching, he hefts out a photograph album.

'This was a few years ago,' he says as he places the album flat on the table between us. 'The diocesan retreat. We went to the Catskills.'

He turns the plastic pages: pictures of groups of priests, each group with a younger Bishop Werner at their centre.

'There's Thomas,' he says. 'Recognize him?'

He's pointing to a man at the end of a group of ten. A broad-shouldered, round-faced man wearing an open-neck, red and white check shirt. My breath catches.

'You recognize him?' the bishop asks again.

'Yes. Yes, I do,' I tell him. I'm standing up, out of breath. 'May I please use your telephone? The battery on mine is dead.'

5

Kay is driving into Bayport. She's called Larry and got his mailbox. She didn't leave a message but tried several more times, with the same result. She normally loves this time of year, when Bayport is full of new people, as cottagers from the islands come in for their errands; now everything she sees is alien. She doesn't think she can keep this up.

After two years as a qualified nurse in Toronto General, she began to study psychology at nights. Gavin was five years old and I had just started work as a teacher. Kay became immersed in Freud and Jung; an analyst told her that she had spent her life, including her childhood, caring for other people. With her father dead and her mother unable to face reality, the responsibility had all fallen to Kay. It was as if she was in a role she could not change, facing a future she could not resist. Eight years later, she qualified as an analyst, and ever since, she has been listening to the problems of others.

She pulls in by Mr Amos's and again calls Larry's number; once more she gets his mailbox. The town is buzzing. Mr Echenoz is loading groceries into the back of his pick-up. Keith comes out of the pharmacy, carrying a package, and walks quickly up the sidewalk, right past her. She thought she had left him back in Roger's Quay.

'Keith?'

But Keith just walks on. Puzzled, Kay eases out and drives slowly down to the lake road. Larry's house has a spectacular view over the water. Kay feels a vein throb in her forehead as she goes around to the back door of Larry's house. She peers out to the lake from the empty jetty, but cannot see beyond the bluff of land that protects the little harbour.

Before Larry White came to Bayport, this house was rented to an architect and his wife, with whom Kay and I occasionally socialised during the summer vacation. Kay raps on the screen outside the back door, although she knows that Larry is not at home. As she waits, she looks down over the tidy plot which he has already prepared for vegetables, and, beyond it, to the untroubled skin of the inlet. Stillness and peace. As she turns to go, she looks again and sees that the back door behind the screen is open.

'Larry?'

On the lake-facing veranda that runs the short length of the house is a rocking chair, a cage with a budgerigar, and a tripod with a mounted telescope. Kay goes to the telescope, removes the viewing cap and puts her eye to the lens. It takes a moment to realize what she is looking at. She gasps. The telescope, pointing at the high tree line to the left of the lakeshore, is trained on our house.

6

A clock ticks on the mantelpiece in the bishop's study. From the front garden the sprinkler sound is audible in wet snatches. Bishop Hal, who has listened intently, interrupting only when points required clarification, now leans forward.

'What a burden you've had to carry all these years.'

'I think Terence has read my book and feels outraged. I think he wants to put the record straight before he dies.'

Bishop Hal reaches for a file and opens it.

'Before we go any further, I have to ask you to promise me that as long as Terence is alive, what I am about to reveal to you remains completely confidential,' he says. 'The contents of this file are highly sensitive and personal – I am only sharing them with you because it may be in Thomas's best interests to do so.'

Our eyes meet. Behind the heavy spectacles, his are deep, dark brown.

'I promise.'

'Very well.' He takes a deep breath. 'Over forty years ago, a young Irishman, Terence Deasy, comes to the United States. He is twenty years of age. He gets a job as a trainee teacher in a Catholic school in Tampa, Florida. His work impresses the Director of Vocations for the diocese and he is invited to apply for admission to the local seminary.'

The bishop adjusts his position in the chair.

'Terence goes through the checks and psychological screening that are in place at the time. These notes hold a few clues to the problems that will later emerge. For example, Terence's childhood in Ireland is surprisingly lacking in detail—he comes from a poor background and has grown up in the care of a state-run institution in County Tipperary, but that's it. A note also says that he complains of sleeping badly and of occasional bad dreams.'

Bishop Werner turns some pages.

'On the positive side, he appears to be a self-sufficient if somewhat tough individual. He is also an intelligent young man, devoted to his religion; in other words, an ideal candidate for a vocation. In the 1970s, the Church is used to recruiting Irish candidates whose backgrounds and hard early circumstances preclude them from the priesthood in Ireland.

'The local bishop admits Terence to the seminary in Tampa. He changes his first name from Terence to Thomas. He is twenty-three years of age.'

The bishop's hip gets the better of him and he stands at the desk, referring to the file.

'In preparation for the priesthood, Thomas studies philosophy and theology, and after three years graduates in these subjects. Five years later he is ordained a priest and begins work in the Tampa area.

'A few years go by before evidence of heavy drinking emerges. Father Deasy is stopped by a routine police patrol and found to be three times over the legal limit.

The police decide to prosecute. Apparently, he has been stopped before but his standing as a popular local priest has persuaded the police not to act. Now he is in trouble. The bishop steps in. He does a deal with the local chief of police: in exchange for Thomas leaving the diocese, the charges will be dropped. Thomas is transferred to Detroit, which is when I first come to know him.'

Bishop Hal smiles.

'Thomas is a compassionate man. Congregations love him, the sick and the dying adore him. He's a good priest but he drinks too much. A few years after he arrives here, a new problem arises. In divorce proceedings between parishioners of this diocese, a husband alleges that his wife has being conducting extra-marital affairs with, among others, a Catholic priest. Thomas is the priest.

'In those days you could keep things out of the papers, which is what happens. The diocese pays a sum of money to the husband and the matter is dropped.

'Thomas claims that drinking has clouded his judgement. He is suspended by my predecessor and agrees to enter a rehabilitation programme, which will also include in-depth psychological analysis. He stays in rehab for three months and quits the booze. When he comes out, he is given duties administering to the sick in local hospitals. During this period, he also works as chaplain in a local prison for young offenders.'

The bishop stoops to the file.

'The doctors' psychological analysis is unanimous: Thomas Deasy should never have become a priest.'

7

Kay cannot stop trembling, and yet, as if she is homing in, inch by inch, on a truth that will not be avoided, she is unable to leave.

'Larry?'

She can see dishes and a cup, a saucepan by the stove. As she pushes in the door the caged bird begins to chirp. Her head pounds. The kitchen is warm and recent cooking smells linger. Kay looks around. She cannot now remember what hung on these walls when the architect and his wife were here, but several framed photographs of Larry stare at her, his big face smiling out from a snowscape, beside a skidoo.

She is walking a precipice; if she stops, she will topple. Her lips stumble over an old prayer: please let Tim be safe. She thinks about calling me, but realizes that her phone is in the car. At the sink, she pauses. Why has Larry left his door open? Does he *want* her to come in? If he does, it means he knew she was coming. She makes herself sit at the kitchen table. She is looking for an explanation, although to what she cannot say. Something in here will tie Larry to recent events. The bedroom door is to one side of the fireplace; Kay goes to it and looks in. A big, square and wooden-framed bed with a headboard fashioned from a split log of local cedar dominates the room. She turns.

'Oh!'

On the chimney breast hangs a blown-up photograph of Larry in his role in last year's Christmas play. Kay gapes. Made up to be the Ghost of Christmas Past, Larry is very pale and suddenly familiar. Kay leans on the bedpost. Across the bed, near the window, a bedside light sits on a pine locker. Kay edges past the bed. Coins lie on the locker, and a partly used foil card of pills. Larry's private life. A slim, leather briefcase is propped by the locker. She lifts the flap. A desk diary, spine upwards, some magazines. Kay lifts out the diary, places it on the bed and opens it. Today's date is marked by a brown envelope which is postmarked Charlton. The envelope is addressed to

Alex Smyth
Author
Bayport
Lake Muskoka
Ontario

8

The bishop all at once looks much older.

'The psychologists report that Thomas seems to have retreated into a childlike world, a wistful, sad place which he is unable to discuss in any detail. More than that, they say that his childhood experience has become what they call "discontinuous". In other words, he cannot provide a full narrative history of his own childhood. Thomas displays all the symptoms of someone whose young life has been interrupted by severe trauma. In such circumstances, the injured person erects psychological defences that allow his life to go on but at great internal cost. Such people are often outwardly tough and resilient and project an aura of self-sufficiency, but in reality this aura conceals a secret dependency, which in Thomas's case is mani-fested in alcohol.'

The bishop pours himself a glass of water. He reads aloud:

"Thomas is prone to regular panic attacks, reports terrifying nightmares and his prevailing mood is one of defeat and hopelessness. He sometimes says that he grew up too soon and that he hates himself."

'And then one day, the dam bursts. Thomas tells his

doctor how he has, since the age of five, been routinely sexually abused by his parish priest in Ireland. The abuse has taken place at night, under the guise of fishing trips. This horror has gone on for over four years until, in another tragedy, the uncle who reared Thomas hangs himself. Thomas is not allowed to attend the funeral, but is put into an institution for children in Clonmel, a sort of workhouse or juvenile jail, where he remains until he reaches the age of seventeen.'

I wonder if there is any mercy in the world.

'He confronted the truth,' I say, 'which is more than I did.'

'The truth is cruel,' Bishop Hal says. 'He has been covering it up for so long that he appears to himself like a stranger. Apparently, this is not unusual, but that doesn't make it any easier. He feels he is in the wrong place. He tells me that he realizes he should never have become a priest.'

Sadness has taken hold of Bishop Hal's face.

'But he is a priest and has no place else to go. He is off the drink. We are short-staffed at the time, so Thomas is admitted back into parish work just after I become bishop.

'Then, a couple of years ago, a new problem emerges.'

The bishop goes to the window that overlooks his rose garden.

'An anonymous letter is received in the chancery that alleges Thomas is in an improper relationship with a woman in the neighbourhood. I wasn't born yesterday. We are all sinners, and there are priests who conduct discreet affairs that don't affect their ability to minister. Frankly, they're not breaking the civil law; the people involved are consenting adults. And yet, celibacy is an iron law of the Church. A priest who openly abandons celibacy cannot remain a priest, otherwise he would give scandal. The woman Thomas is seeing comes from Costa Rica, is about half his age and is living in the United States illegally. Her name is Maria.'

The bishop is silhouetted by the bright window.

'I call him in and confront him. He doesn't deny it. I tell him that he knows the rules; that this cannot go on. He says he is just trying to help Maria with her immigration problems. She is a good Catholic, he says.

'One thing leads to another. There are people in this world, I'm sure you know them, Alex, whose righteousness can only be expressed in exposing the sins of others. A group of parishioners make it their mission to have Maria deported back to Costa Rica as an undocumented immigrant. She is forced to give up her apartment. She is mysteriously laid off from her job as a cleaner in a local dentist's surgery. Thomas is distraught. In an attempt to stop Maria's forcible deportation, he moves her into his house in Saint Patrick's.'

Bishop Hal's head sinks.

'This is the final straw. I cannot permit a priest to live openly on church property with a woman. I give him an ultimatum, but he ignores me. I suspend him. He and Maria move out, into an apartment which he pays for. I expect then that he will leave the priesthood and marry Maria. In fact, I really hope that he will! Thomas is a man who needs a physical relationship and if leaving the priesthood and marrying will bring him peace and happiness at last, who am I not to wish him well and support him in this new phase of his life?'

'But it was not to be.'

'Less than a week later, when Thomas is away from their apartment, Maria is arrested and deported to Costa Rica. Poor Thomas! He wants to follow her, but there are no details of where she can be found. The deportation people refuse to help him. He makes no attempt to return to his house in Saint Patrick's or to seek my advice. He starts drinking again.'

Sixty years later and still he cannot escape.

'He is admitted to ER on several occasions with head injuries from falling when he was drunk,' the bishop says. 'I try my very best to have him readmitted to rehab, but he refuses. Then, nine months or so ago, on yet another admission to ER, he is diagnosed with terminal oesophageal cancer. His medical insurance from the diocese covers his treatment. Then a month ago, he disappeared. I have no idea where he is. He's a big strong man, as you know. A fighter. But when I got your call, I thought it might be to tell me he is dead.'

9

The lake brightens with the transit of the sun as Kay sits in our kitchen, waiting. She has come to a point where she can think of only a few simple facts, and these she clings to, like someone dreaming and re-dreaming the same images: I'm on my way home; Larry White is in possession of a letter addressed to me with a fish hook in it; Tim is out on the lake with Larry White. My message on her cell phone merely said that everything was all right and I would explain later. And yet what she has just found in Larry's house has made her dysfunctional. She snatches up the phone and calls Keith.

'It's Kay Smyth.'

'Yes, Mrs Smyth?'

'Has Tim come in yet?'

'No, ma'am, but like I said, they're going back to Mr White's—'

'I know what you said, Keith, and I went there and they haven't come back. Look, I need Tim here *now*. Urgently. His, ah, father is calling from China to speak to him. I want you to get in a boat and go out and bring him back here.'

'I can call Mr White,' Keith suggests.

'I've tried and he doesn't answer! Now go out there, please, and bring him back! Tell him it's an emergency.'

As she sits there, shaking, thinking that she should have asked Keith to do that an hour ago, she's lighting another cigarette when the phone rings. She grabs it.

'Alex?' She can hear breathing. 'Hello?'

'Is Alex Smyth there?' A man's voice, an Irishman.

'I'm sorry, Alex's not here—who's calling?'

A long pause.

'This is Kay Smyth, Alex's wife. Who's calling please?'

It's as if he is struggling to find another word.

'Is there something wrong?' she asks. 'Who are you?'

She can hear him, although he doesn't speak.

10

The bishop and I walk back out through his house.

'I believe he's in Canada, in Muskoka,' I say. 'When I first got the hook he sent through the mail, I was terrified, but now I just want to meet him and tell him I'm sorry.'

'You were two kids,' Bishop Werner says. 'Neither of you did anything wrong. Fear lies in the unknown, in what we have hidden from ourselves. You and Thomas were no different.'

'Is it possible to get a copy of that picture you showed me?'

'I'll photograph it with my phone,' says Bishop Hal. 'Do you have an email address?'

We pause by the door with its motifs of moons and stars.

'I'm sure you could have done without me dumping my problems on you,' I say. 'I apologise.'

'Please, no need,' the bishop says. 'You see, I already knew your story.'

I'm staring at him.

'Oh, yes,' he says with a sad smile. 'Thomas told me everything.'

Kat sits, holding the phone.

'Who is this?' she asks again.

The man says: 'My name is Father Seán Phelan and I'm phoning from Ireland.'

Her first reaction is that there has been an accident.

'Has something happened? Is Alex all right?'

'I'm sorry, I didn't mean to give you a fright. I just want to talk to him.'

Of course, she thinks, dizzily, he has already asked to speak to Alex.

'Alex is away, Father. Can I help you?'

Another pause.

'But he should be back later today. He's been in Ireland.'

'I know.'

During each silence, she wonders if he's hung up.

'Did Alex meet you, Father Phelan? In the last couple of days?'

'Yes.'

'You must know each other.'

'Yes, we were at school together. And in the seminary.'

'So you're old friends.'

As he hesitates again, Kay suddenly knows that something vital has led to this call.

'Father Phelan, you can talk to me,' she says. 'It's fine to talk.'

It's such a lengthy pause that she reckons she has indeed lost him. She wills him to keep going.

'Year and years ago, when I was only seven years of age… '

'Go on, Father.'

'…I used to serve Mass here for the parish priest. His name was Father Charles McVee.'

13

Kay has been sitting for thirty minutes. Once Father Seán Phelan began, he could not stop. Kay heard a lifetime's pain, decades of agony pouring out, as the priest explained how he had twice lacked the courage to tell the truth: once, over forty years ago, in a pub on Woodstown Beach; and again a few days before, when I had gone to his house outside Carrick. Now, haltingly, he described what had been done to him in the church sacristy, and also in the Phelans' home, where Father McVee was a regular for Sunday lunch.

'Part of me believed it had never happened,' he said, 'but that was the part of me that didn't want to believe it. My parents thought he was a saint.'

It takes a whole lifetime to come to terms with what we have hidden as children, Kay knows.

'I could have helped Alex that day in Woodstown,' said Father Phelan, 'because I knew immediately what he was talking about. But to have helped him would have meant bringing shame on myself and that is something I have never been brave enough to do.'

'You are being brave now, Father,' Kay said. 'Very brave.'

'Tell Alex I'm sorry. Tell him my whole life has been a lie.'

When the call is over, Kay makes herself go about household tasks, even though she doesn't know where she will find the energy. She is sorry now that she ever doubted me, she will later say, for the call from Father Phelan has changed everything in a way that she well understands: the past is finally being run to ground.

Unfolding the ironing board, she sets it up, plugs in the iron and hauls out a basket of clothes. As she tries to concentrate on laying out a shirt on the board, she hears a car's engine. Her breath is trapped in her chest as she stands there and a man's shadow suddenly appears on the window.

Larry White opens the door and walks in. He's wearing shorts, deck shoes and a lightweight open jacket over a t-shirt that emphasises his physique. His dark hair is wet and slicked back. Tim, the top of his wetsuit still on, is behind him. Kay forces herself to be calm.

'Hi, Larry.'

'Kay, what's the problem?' Larry makes a quick survey, checking left and right, up the stairs. 'Keith said there's some kind of emergency.'

She can't help being drawn to the glaring smoothness running from his left temple to his jaw. A few weeks ago she looked forward to seeing this man; now she's terrified of him.

'I needed Tim,' she says lightly. 'His dad's due to call. Thanks for bringing him back here. But now…'

'Quite a little champ you got in the making here,' Larry says, taking off his jacket. 'He'll be on just one ski before you know it.'

Kay busies herself with the ironing board, folding it away. 'Larry, can you excuse us, please? Maybe another time?'

'Mr White says this is his most favourite house in Bayport,' Tim says.

'After my own, remember?' Larry says.

'Tim,' Kay says steadily, 'I want you to go to your bedroom.'

'Grandma?' The child is still in thrall to his recent lake adventure. 'It's the daytime.'

'Go to your room,' she says firmly. 'Now.'

Tim, bewildered, but a little scared too since she so seldom speaks to him like that, goes up the stairs. Larry is holding his jacket, frowning.

'This is not a good time, Larry,' Kay says pointedly. 'Please.'

'Hey, I want to tell you about Tim.'

'It will have to keep.'

'I don't understand.'

She shakes her head. 'Look, I'm not feeling too good, okay? So please just go.'

'Let me help you.' He takes a step forward. 'Sit down, Kay. Let me get you a glass of water.'

'No. Go, please.'

'Hey,' he says and puts a chair beside her. 'Sit down, Kay. You look like you've seen a ghost.'

Kay sits, trying to compose herself. Larry is drawing up another chair.

'You can talk to me,' he says.

'Grandma?' Tim has re-emerged and is standing on the stairs.

'Tim,' Kay says, 'I told you to go to your room. *Do*

203

it!' She stands, her breath short, until she hears the bedroom door click. 'Larry, this is my house. I need my space.'

'I've just spent an hour water-skiing with your grandson,' Larry says with a big, engaging smile; 'I think I'm due some kind of explanation.'

'There's nothing to explain. I just want to be on my own.'

'And I want you to calm down and listen,' Larry says and stands up. 'Whatever it is, I can help you. There's obviously something wrong.' He reaches for her. 'Please… '

'No!' She stumbles back, three or four paces, into the kitchen. 'I want you to leave.'

Larry follows coolly, like someone for whom this kind of situation is not unusual. 'Not until you tell me what's going on.' His attitude has acquired an unyielding set to it. She sees the muscle in his jaw twitching. 'Are you in some kind of trouble, Kay?'

'No!'

'I'm not so sure about that.' He takes another step forward.

Kay's fingers fumble for the kitchen scissors. 'Get out!' She points the scissors. 'Don't touch me!'

Larry is circling warily. 'You're crazy. I would never harm you. Do you not understand? I worship you.'

'Oh Jesus.'

'From the first day I saw you.'

'Who are you really, Larry?' Kay gasps. 'Where have you come from? And why is there an envelope addressed to my husband in the locker beside your bed?'

204

Larry lets out a slow breath, as if these are indeed big questions.

'Okay,' he says. 'Okay, I can explain.'

'You were at my window that night in Charlton,' she says. 'That was you, wasn't it?'

'No way would I do that.'

'I don't believe you!'

'Kay, I want you to put down the scissors,' he says. Once more he looks around. 'Is it Alex? Is Alex here? Is he threatening you?'

Kay screams, as loudly as she can. Larry falls back a step, as if she's hit him. The telephone rings.

'Kay, give me the scissors.'

The telephone rings and rings.

'Aren't you going to answer it?' Larry says.

Kay reaches to the phone on the wall, the scissors still held out rigid.

'Hello?'

'Kay, it's me,' I say.

PART FIVE

Ontario, Canada

Two years ago

1

We're sitting in the sun on the porch with a pitcher of Kay's home-made lemonade. Nearby someone is cutting a lawn: the constant engine sound in the middle distance rises and falls over our little community, tying us all to this place on a Sunday morning.

Earlier, Gavin called from China, and he and Tim spoke for nearly an hour. Now I hear the thump of a football and see our grandchild throw his hands triumphantly in the air.

What struck me forcibly yesterday in Detroit, when I saw the bishop's photograph, was how little Terence had changed. In his red-and-white-checked shirt, standing on the edge of that happy group in the Catskills, I could still see the shape and cut of the boy who had grown into the man. I nearly cried when I saw him, for he could have been no one else. In his own way, he had eventually done what he had planned so many years ago on Flannery's farm: to sail away, like Robinson Crusoe—in this case, to America, a land where almost no one knows anyone.

This morning, I have explained everything to Kay, as best I can, beginning with those days of my childhood when Charlie McVee's shadow fell over our lives. Within the confines of my promise to the bishop, I have told her all that I can about Terence, including my belief that he read my book and was hurt by what it did not contain. Until this morning, when we spoke, we had not discussed the fly hook he sent me in the mail. Terence knew the coachman would mean more than any letter—and he was right. I did him wrong once and I did him wrong again in my novel, by leaving him out. Now he has cancer, and may well be dead.

We agree that the man at her window that night was probably a vagrant, in off the street in Charlton, looking for a place to spend the night. And any kid Tim's age, having just seen a policeman assembling an Identikit of a suspect stalker, would be bound to see faces like that everywhere he looked. That's what we agree.

Kay is still recovering from her confrontation with Larry. Although she now thinks that she over-reacted to his appearance yesterday, and that Tim was not in any danger from him, it's clear that Larry is not just the helpful ex-cop we once thought he was. In his over-the-top zealousness to protect her—which itself arose from an inappropriate interest—he behaved outrageously, entering our home and removing the most recent correspondence he could find from my office, apparently for the purpose of getting my fingerprints, or so he told Kay last evening, before he eventually left. He wanted to see if I had a record of domestic violence, he told her.

I'm going to let a few weeks go by, just to let everything simmer down; then I'll have a chat with him. You have to be careful how you deal with people in a small community like ours. As I said to Kay, although Larry was way out of line, we too were at fault, convincing ourselves that he might be Terence.

I'm weary following my trip, and more than a little distressed by what I saw and learned in Ireland. A good lifetime has taken place in Canada, whereas in Ireland, during that same span, nothing seems to have changed. Kay has told me of her long conversation with Seán Phelan, of his outpouring of the guilt and shame imposed on him by a rotten system. The circumstances in which I found him—a virtual prisoner in his own house, ever fearful of the tide he feels turning against him, still terrified to tell me the truth—were so symbolic of his internal captivity. Even forty years ago he had used alcohol as his only means of escape.

It is a tragedy too that my father did not have it in him to forgive me. That would have required a miracle, not the walking on water kind of miracle, but the more profound kind, the miracles that take place deep within us. What drives my father, even to this day? What holds the doctor so captive that he cannot even bear to look at me? Is it someone I remind him of that makes it so painful? Does he look at me and see my mother? Or when he sees me, is he sucked down to a place much darker than I will ever know?

Kay sits back, her head tilted to the sun. We thought what we'd come through together years ago had prepared us for anything, but we were wrong. Life, for me at least, can never be taken for granted: the moment I sat back and fooled myself that my life was under control, like some animal I thought I had tamed, it whipped around and bit me.

'Let's take the boat out later,' I say. 'I'll make a picnic.'

Her drowsy smile. It's going to be okay.

A stack of stuff has piled up in my office; besides, I need to plan a trip to see my agent in Toronto. My head is light as I make my way inside.

2

I have read that the less you look at a computer screen, the better for your health; I write in longhand with a silver fountain pen, purchased many years ago in Dublin, a thick, ribbed instrument that connects my brain to the paper, at my speed. I remove the pen from its case, get out a yellow pad and switch on my pc. My aversion to reading from the screen extends to emails and their attachments, all of which I print out.

I want to write down all the little details of this last week, including such items as the colour of the farmer's wife's hair in Flannery's, and how that farm has changed from the way it used to be, as well as the humpy, moss-covered hillocks that stand in front of our old house on the Suir where once the beech trees stood. Energy is coursing through me. I feel like someone who has learned to fly.

A row of emails download, including the minutes of the last meeting of past teachers from Saint Celestine's, which I missed. I open it and print it. One by one I go down the mails: one from Mr Amos, announcing his retirement, which is a matter of regret; a request from Jerry Fisher for permission to give my address to a magazine in Montreal that wants to contact me.

A dozen unwanted mails from companies selling holidays, stationery and medicines, all of which I delete. A mail from Chancellery Saint Patrick's, with a message saying, 'FYA' and an attachment. I open it and press print, then return to my pen and yellow pad.

How can I write a story that will, in essence, reveal *Sulphur* as a fake? The broad nib with its lovely dark ink runs across the page, leaving behind the curled words of my life. I sit back, wondering. Something in this doesn't quite fit, as if not all the truth has come to light, as if a central fact has been omitted. Looking outside, I can tell by the light that it's noon, which means that I'd better make that picnic. I take up the print-out from Chancellery Saint Patrick's and read it as I walk towards the kitchen.

Kay is outside, wearing a straw hat and gardening gloves. She's taking out dead growth from a border.

'Where's Tim?' I ask.

'Keith dropped by and he went with him over to Roger's.'

'Keith? He went to Roger's with Keith?'

'Yes—I said we'd pick him up there when we go for our picnic. What is it, Alex?'

'Get in the car.'

214

3

Kay is still wearing her gardening gloves and hat; I'm still gripping the print-out as I wheel out on to the road and point for the lake.

'In nineteen seventy-nine, when Father Thomas Deasy was working in Detroit, he spent five months as relief chaplain in the juvenile correction facility in Chatham, Ontario.'

The corner of the lake comes into view.

'Chatham is where Keith was in prison,' I say.

'Oh, God,' Kay says, 'does that mean . . .?'

'I don't know what it means. The man at your window, the man outside the house. Now this connection—I think I know where Terence is.'

Seen through the pine trees, the lake is a blinding white as we pull up at Roger's Quay. I'm still holding the page and praying to the God I have so often offended. Mr Amos is walking towards us down the wooden dock.

'Jacob, you seen Keith?'

Mr Amos closes one eye as he surveys me. 'Went out 'bout an hour ago. Maybe more.'

'Was our grandson with him? Tim? He's eight years old. Was Tim in the boat?'

'Couldn't rightly say. You folks okay?'

'We're fine,' I hear myself say as I run along the jetty with Kay behind me. 'Check the repairs shed!' I shout as I jump down into the *Maid of Kerry*.

Within a minute, I have the engine running and the painter ready to cast off.

'Shed's locked,' Kay says, climbing in.

Foam churns at our stern as we make our way out from Roger's at well in excess of regulation. At the mouth of the creek, I push the throttle as far forward as it will go and the boat sits back into herself.

'Where is Tim?' Kay asks.

'He's gone with Keith. They've gone out to Terence.'

Kay is open-mouthed. 'Gone out? Where? These lakes are vast.'

'They've gone to Hermit's Island. I'm pretty sure Terence Deasy is there. Keith has been looking after him, feeding him, bringing him medicines.'

'How do you know?'

'I just know.'

'Is Tim all right?'

I feel confidence beyond reason when I say, 'Tim is absolutely fine.'

4

We've settled into a rhythmic flight northwards across the smooth water. We've both tried to call Tim and Keith, but neither is picking up. To our port side, the shoreline falls away, revealing inlets where the gardens of cottages come down to the lake. The launch thuds water as the outline of islands appears in the distance. I know now that the final part of this story is about to fall into place. That in itself is terrifying, since there is a dark line in my imagination that I do not want to cross. We keep a steady course in mid-channel. Some of the islands are uninhabited rock outcrops, smothered in vegetation; others have a single dwelling set in pine trees and overlooking neatly painted moorings. We swing into another part of the lake, a place I'm not too familiar with. This great body of water runs to over two thousand square miles.

'Look!'

Kay is pointing to figures on a spit of land. It's our neighbour, Dimitri Echenoz, with a group of kids. I head in and swing broadside to the shore, about twenty yards out.

'Alex, Kay, come on in and have a drink!' Dimitri shouts.

'Thanks, maybe later,' I call back. 'Dimitri—have you seen Keith or Tim?'

'Sure, Keith went by earlier. Tim was with him.'

'Which way were the headed?'

'Which way was Keith headed?' Dimitri turns to a child. 'Pierre?'

Pierre wears spectacles. 'They were headed for Hermit's,' he says, peering at us. 'Tim says there's some old sick guy there.'

'Tim told you that?' his father says. It's clear from Dimitri's reaction that he hasn't heard this before. 'Are you sure?'

'Sure I'm sure,' Pierre says. 'Tim's been out couple of times to see him.'

I hit the throttle.

The lake widens and after fifteen minutes the outline of a solitary outcrop grows into view. Hermit's Island is just a few defiant glacial acres, a place where kids sometimes party and where some years back contraband smugglers were run to ground. The water arc on either side of the spray hood subsides as I kill the engine, take out paddles and hand one to Kay. We glide in to a beach of shale.

'I don't know what we're going to find here,' I say, 'but it may be tough to take.'

'I can take tough,' Kay says.

We wade knee-deep for ten yards. I love Kay in a way that is new, as if today's capacity to surprise is endless, as if my life will always be nurtured by that vital first moment on the strand in Tramore when our eyes met. The terrain is uneven and the scrub of the island dense as we edge through on ever-rising ground. Light is failing and the blue-black sky is unmarked and flawless. Kay points. Where the sun meets aluminium, it shines white as a spotlight.

We begin a long, crouching diversion. A hierarchy of dread engulfs me, with an image of my grandson's dead body at its summit. I know this cannot happen and yet I know it happens every day. After several hundred yards, twenty yards from the lakeshore, the little creek where Keith's boat has been slid in under the vegetation is in front of us. All at once I can smell something.

'Tobacco,' Kay whispers.

Cigarette scent lies on the still air and makes me think of the days when patients smoked in the doctor's waiting room. A rocky outcrop blocks our way, but when we round it, fifty yards farther on I see three seated figures, their faces to the east. Keith and Tim are smoking cigarettes. Between them, head slumped, is a man. He's been wedged into a rock under a rough hoop of birch branches. Keith is chanting in a low, mournful voice. Tim, to my amazement, is smoking his cigarette with relish.

Part Six

Ontario, Canada

Present Day

1

Through the emerald branches of hemlock, I can glimpse the sunlight on Lake Muskoka. Summer has come early to Ontario, something everyone says is because of climate change. Beavers and racoons can be seen on the islands, and white-tailed deer are grazing the groves of alder and birch along the foreshore. Bright sunlight pierces the foliage of the oak tree where the blue jay has taken up position. Down on the water there's bound to be a good hatch tonight.

It's a midweek morning and Jerry Fisher is due from Toronto. My agent's enthusiasm over these last weeks has made my blood quicken. He has secured a deal for my second novel, and is now hopeful for translation rights in Europe. As Jerry puts it: 'We need to launch you in the non-English-speaking world'.

Tim has grown up a lot recently, which reminds me of myself when I was nearly ten years of age. He's being driven up here by his father to stay with us for a week and go fishing; from where I sit at my desk, with the view of the lake, every time I hear a car I look up to see if it's them.

My father's health began to deteriorate sharply a year ago; one day the nursing home in Waterford called.

'He has asked for you,' Nurse Mary said.

When I heard that, I was sad, but sadness is something I have learned to cope with.

'He has a few days left, a week at the most,' she said.

'I will pray for him,' I said.

So I did, by the side of a trout-filled lake that the doctor had never seen. He died on a Wednesday morning when Ireland was in the grip of a great storm, I later learned. By his own request, he was taken to the parish church in south Tipperary where he and I had knelt and prayed so many times, and was then brought to the adjoining cemetery where my mother lies, as do Mr and Mrs Flannery. His funeral Mass was said by the parish priest, Father Seán Phelan, Nurse Mary wrote. There was a good turnout and Father Phelan's eulogy was uplifting. He told the congregation that Paddy Smyth was a wonderful man who had dedicated his life to the healing of others and, having lived for more than nine decades, had now been taken to his heavenly reward. My father's few belongings could be forwarded to me, if I wished, Nurse Mary said. They amounted to no more than his clothes and the contents of his bedside locker.

Her letter enclosed a snapshot, found among my father's possessions, of him and my mother, around the time of their marriage, taken by a street photographer in Waterford. They turn around at the moment the photographer calls to them. Hope and laughter shine from their young faces. It is terrifying to think of what lay ahead.

2

Another letter, sent to my publisher, and then forwarded to Jerry Fisher, arrived a month after my father's death. The writer, whose each pen stroke was transcribed with an almost artistic flourish, signed himself as Brother Malachy, Wilkins Abbey. He began by explaining how he had been trying to find a way of contacting me. He went on to say that, following my departure that day from the Abbey, he had gone back to his cell and come upon some old notes he had made of his conversations with Father Charlie McVee.

Brother Malachy did not wish to cause me pain by bringing up the past again, he wrote, but nonetheless, since we had discussed in some detail what had been the deceased priest's state of mind, he felt he should relay one of their final conversations.

'I asked him if he regretted what he had done, but he just looked at me with what I can only describe as defiance. I reminded him that he had not much longer to live. He shrugged. I then asked him: in the event of his not being fearful for himself, was he not fearful for his soul? He looked at me, as if there were some things I would never understand. Then he said: "The body is just a playground, Malachy. It is nothing. All this...

this trouble is nothing! The soul doesn't bother with any of that. The soul swims through all those nets and into the big lake of God's mercy.'"

With a silent prayer of thanks to the guiding spirit that had brought me to Kay, I glanced once more at the blue stationery with its calligraphy; then I balled up the letter and threw it in the fire.

3

I have spoken on the telephone a few times to Seán Phelan over the last two years. He's a lonely, decent man who, like me, has spent his adult life suffering wounds inflicted in his childhood. He's looking forward to retiring, he says. He wants to travel. His sister lives in Australia and her husband has died. There's so much of the world he hasn't seen, Seán says.

Keith still works in Roger's Quay; he continues to service my boat. He had been nursing Father Thomas Deasy for over a week on Hermit's Island. The priest had refused to go into the emergency department of Charlton Hospital, or to the Catholic priest in that town. He had only a short time to live, he knew, and told Keith that he wanted to spend those days somewhere on the lake. He said that it reminded him of Ireland. Keith said that Father Thomas was one of the few people who had treated him decently in the juvenile correction centre in Chatham, and that Father Thomas was his friend.

The priest had wanted to meet me, Keith said, but was afraid of how I might react to his request. The drugs he was taking, including painkillers, had unbalanced him and he was prone to periods of hallucination. The night he appeared at Kay's window in Charlton hospital, he had been attending the emergency department. The priest cried a lot, Keith told me, and when Keith asked him if he was in pain, he said, yes, but not the kind of pain anyone might imagine.

When he learned about Tim, Terence asked to be allowed see the child and talk to him.

I never did get to have that chat with Larry White. He left Bayport some weeks after these events without saying goodbye. We never met again, so who he really was remains a mystery to this day. I heard much later from several people who are close to the police in Charlton that Larry was once a narcotics officer in Vancouver, working undercover, and that he'd come to Bayport to find a new life when the drugs gang in which he was embedded discovered his true identity; but maybe that was just a rumour.

Terence's body was taken to Charlton. Kay and I arranged a church, and Bishop Hal Werner said the funeral Mass. Keith was the only other person to attend. The bishop took the ashes back to Saint Patrick's, Detroit, where there is a plot beside the chancellery for deceased priests of the diocese.

4

Tim is a fine boy, big-boned like me, good-looking like his father and his grandmother. Sometimes we go fishing along the lakeshore, or from *Maid of Kerry*. Tim's got a deft touch with a fly rod that I never had; but I've started to fish with him anyway. It relaxes me and I'm getting better at it. My days with Tim on the lake are spent checking out the best spots for trout, and when we go back home, we leaf through the latest magazines and discuss the merits of different types of flies.

On the evening that Terence died on Hermit's Island, when we got home, I sat down with Tim. Just the two of us.

'Keith brought me out twice before to see his sick friend,' he told me. 'He was real nice. Keith was cooking for him, but he wouldn't eat. Keith made me promise to tell no one about him.'

Keith had been buying medicines and bringing them out to Hermit's Island.

'He said his name was Terence. Said he knew you well—that you had been friends once. Were you once his friend, granddad?'

'Yes, I was.'

It had become dark outside, the kind of early summer dark that folds you into it and keeps you warm. Tim told me how he had been kicking a ball on the lawn when Keith pulled up.

'He asked me if I'd like to come and help him,' Tim said. 'I kind of knew where we were going.'

They drove to Roger's where Keith fired up his biggest boat and they went straight out to Hermit's. Terence was lying beside a fire, wrapped in blankets. He had become extremely weak.

'He says he wants to tell you stuff,' Keith told Tim.

Tim had to kneel down to hear.

'He asked me questions.'

'About?'

'Whether I had ever been to Ireland. Whether Great-Granddad Smyth had ever come over here. If I had ever met him.'

The child turned to me.

'Asked if you and I fished here on Muskoka. I told him you didn't fish much, but that I water-skied.'

'That was a good answer.'

'He told me about how his mom had died and how his uncle, who was a kind man, had taken him in. They lived on a farm and had their own river—imagine their own river!'

'Quite a river too.'

'Keith was trying to get him to take his medication, but Terence didn't want to. Sometimes he closed his eyes and I thought he was asleep, but then he'd start whispering again. He told me how he'd learned to fish for trout. How the best fish were always caught at night.'

I began to discern the outline of a purpose, as if the dead man was using Tim to give me information.

'What else did he tell you?'

'How he often went down to the river at night with the priest and the doctor. Lots of times. He said I should tell you that.'

'He said that?'

'He said it was very important.'

'What did he say then?'

'That the priest took him to a special place to fish, on his own,' Tim said.

'And the doctor?'

'He went to another place,' Tim said. 'But Terence said the doctor knew.'

I didn't care if my grandson saw my tears.

'He said that?'

'Yes. He said that when I met you, I should tell you that. What did he mean, Granddad? What did the doctor know?'

It is often said that the dying can hear much more than is supposed. It is reported by those who have come back from the brink that, despite their seeming deadness, even when their heart has stopped, they are vividly aware of people around them. Some describe it as swimming into the darkness, like a little fish. They can hear the water lapping gently as they move ever farther, as the deeper and deeper currents take them into their care, as they let go and the shore recedes, as the noise and harshness of the land is forgotten and bit by bit they become one with the mystery of the water and the music of the night.